THE WHEELCHAIR

and Other Stories

THE WHEELCHAIR

and Other Stories

THEODORE DALRYMPLE

MIRABEAU PRESS

Published by Mirabeau Press

PO Box 4281

West Palm Beach, FL 33401

ISBN: 978-1-7357055-4-5

First Edition

MIRABEAU

CONTENTS

The Wheelchair...1

The War of the Roses...23

Getting to the Roots 44

The Sting 71

Redressing the Balance...89

Punctuation Mark 105

Parting of the Waters 121

The Restaurant Trade 141

THE WHEELCHAIR

Leopoldo Smith, widower, was a man unremarkable in all respects but his name, in which his drunken father, in a state of inebriation, had registered him at birth, thinking it a good joke. Everyone called him Leo, of course. Until his retirement at the age of sixty-five, he had been a postman and nothing else. He was born at a time when lack of ambition was not regarded as a defect of character, and he had never sought advancement of any kind. His wife Betty had borne him no children, and they had accepted their childlessness with resignation. Leo was not religious in any formal sense, but he believed vaguely, without giving it much thought, in a higher power usually designated as God, and if that higher power decreed that he should have no children, who was he, mere Leo Smith, to question it?

Betty had died five years ago of a condition about which she refused to consult a doctor until it was too late. Leo had then to learn the domestic skills, or activities, that until then he had sub-contracted to her, so to speak. He performed them with indifferent success: his clothes now always had a crumpled appearance, and if he ate a boiled egg, some of its yolk was certain to find its way down his front, nearly as far as his feet, leaving its trace until his next washday. His week had two high points: on Wednesdays he would go to a nearby café for a slap-up breakfast, and on Friday evenings he would go for a quiet pint to the Cock and Feathers, where he was known but not much spoken to, and he left before the raucousness began. He bought a newspaper three times a week, the least intellectual of the genre, the type that announced in big headlines that Adolf Hitler had been found and was living on the far side of the moon. Leo believed it because it had been in the papers.

He never stopped to consider whether he was happy, or whether he might be happier if things were different. Life for him was a given: it was simply accepted as it was and had somehow to be got through.

His little house was one of a terrace of precisely such houses that abutted on a main road which, though it was only two lanes wide, was still an important commercial route between two larger towns in the district. A much wider road, that avoided Leo's town altogether, had been projected but for budgetary reasons not so far built (the constituency of which the town was a part was a safe seat, not having changed party hands for ninety years); for this reason, fifty-ton trucks continued to thunder through the town causing earth tremors, behemoths by comparison with the houses. They never slowed, as if they had not noticed that they were passing through an inhabited area. There seemed to be scores of them, and each made the windows of the houses rattle.

On one of the days on which Leo went to fetch his newspaper from the little shop on the corner owned by Mr Patel (whose son was studying biochemistry at Oxford), he emerged from his front door just as an articulated truck was passing. It was a wet and blustery day, the road and the stones of the narrow pavement in front of the terrace glistened with the rain. The truck was driven at a speed that did not acknowledge the existence of the town. There was a sudden gust of wind as the truck passed Leo, and its flatbed swayed and swung. Some part of it caught him a glancing blow. The truck sped on, the driver oblivious of what he had done; Leo was left sprawling on the ground, his leg twisted and broken. There were no witnesses and there was no one about to help. He had never suffered such agony in seventy years.

Several cars went by without stopping, their drivers assuming, if they saw him, that the man on the pavement was an early morning drunk, or still suffering the consequences of gross overindulgence the night before. Leo was waving feebly for assistance; his calls for help travelled only a few inches from his mouth. Eventually, however, a car stopped, its driver impelled by curiosity. It was soon clear to him that Leo was seriously injured, for his trousers were soaked in blood. By now, Leo was in little condition to tell him what had happened, even had he really known it; his few words were incoherent and disjointed.

He was rushed to hospital. Some of his bones were smashed, and a surgeon repaired them as best he could. Afterwards, when Leo came round from the anaesthetic, the surgeon had a little talk with him.

'I've done the best I could for you,' he said. 'But I'm afraid your leg will be somewhat deformed.'

'Will I be able to walk?' asked Leo anxiously.

'With intensive physiotherapy,' said the surgeon. 'But

perhaps not perfectly.'

'How long will I be in plaster?'

The surgeon puckered his mouth to indicate uncertainty.

'It depends on the healing. But at least two months, maybe three.'

Leo was a patient and uncomplaining man even in circumstances in which he had a choice; he always did what he was told, and the nurses could safely ignore or neglect him. He was, however, taught how to use crutches, and by the time he was discharged from the hospital, he could hop a few steps on one leg, his damaged leg in its cast a dead weight, like something that he had laboriously to carry.

'Your wife will be pleased to see you back,' said the senior nurse to him as a porter wheeled his way from the ward to the wating ambulance.

'She's dead,' said Leo.

'Oh, I'm sorry,' said the nurse. 'It says on your admission form that you're married.'

'Widowed,' said Leo.

Everyone had assumed that the reason she had not visited Leo in hospital was that it had been too difficult for her to come: that was the usual reason. The bus service from Leo's town had just been cut for lack of passengers. Besides, at her age and in her social class, it was quite likely that she would be incapacitated.

'Who is there at home, then, to look after you?' asked the nurse.

'No one. A neighbour might help with the shopping, I suppose.'

The nurse was taken aback.

'Why didn't you tell us?'

'You didn't ask.'

There was no reproach in Leo's answer, only information.

'Well now,' said the nurse, faintly exasperated, 'we'll have to arrange something.'

'What?' asked Leo.

'Excuse me,' interjected the porter who was waiting with a wheelchair to take Leo to the vehicle that would take him home, 'Transport's very busy.' He pointed to his watch. 'If he don't come now, he'll lose his slot, and it'll have to get on with the next job.'

'All right, take him,' said the nurse. 'I'll arrange everything from here.'

Everything turned out to be the district nurse who, as she put it, 'popped in' from time to time to check that he was not yet a corpse, and also an appointment with an orthopaedic surgeon (actually, the most junior member of his staff), together with a car to take him to the hospital.

Leo had to live on the ground floor of his little house because he couldn't climb the stairs to his bedroom, the dead weight and awkwardness of his plaster being too much for him. Even downstairs he had to haul himself about on a kitchen chair, a slow, inconvenient and noisy process. He slept on the sofa in the front room that overlooked the road and spent most of his time in watching television or reading his newspaper. It was Mrs Phillips from next door who brought it and who did his shopping for him (he lived mainly on cheese sandwiches). He suspected that Mrs Phillips kept some of his change, though he couldn't be sure; in any case, there was nothing he could do about it, for he was now reliant on her.

Mr Jones, his neighbour on the other side, was ninety and nearly bedbound himself; it was his daughter who looked after him, and Leo could hardly ask her to take on extra responsibilities because she also had a daughter, a single mother, to assist.

'You'll have to be careful not to eat too much, Leo,' the district nurse said to him one day when she saw a plate of cheese sandwiches by his side. 'Because you're not getting any exercise, you could easily put on weight, and then it would be difficult for you to get around. It would retard your rehabilitation.'

'I don't eat much,' said Leo.

'It's not only a question of how much you eat,' said the district nurse, 'but how much energy you use. If the energy you use is less than what there is in your food, it's converted into fat and you put on weight. That puts a strain on your joints and you get arthritis.'

Then she measured his blood pressure.

'It's all right at the moment, but that's another reason not to put on weight.'

Next time she came, or 'popped in', she resumed the subject of diet.

'I don't think you're getting enough fruit and vegetables,' she said. 'You should have five a day.'

'Five a day what?'

'Portions. Fruit and veg. Apples, oranges, raspberries. Broccoli, lettuce, green beans. Tomatoes, that kind of thing. As far as I can see, you just live on sandwiches.'

'I like sandwiches. It's all right.'

'I'm not talking about what you like,' said the district nurse with a laugh, 'but what's good for you. That's what I'm here for.'

Leo didn't know how to prepare vegetables and he had never liked fruit much, other than bananas, and they were bad fruit.

When he went to the hospital, the young surgeon-in-training asked him how he was getting around.

'The crutches are difficult,' said Leo. 'I'm so unsteady on them that I don't use them much.'

'You'll get used to them as time goes on,' said the young surgeon.

'I'd like a wheelchair,' said Leo. 'Then I could get about a bit.'

'I assumed you already had one. You'll have to ask your doctor about that. The hospital doesn't provide them.'

Next day, Leo called the doctor's surgery. It had removed a few years earlier to the edge of town and was built in the style of a pizza chain restaurant. There were ten doctors there, the only ones in the town, but they were never the same ones. They seemed to be always retiring, on maternity leave or moving on to somewhere else.

'Switchboard is very busy today. Please hold and your call will be answered as soon as one of our receptionists becomes available. You are currently number seventeen in the queue. Did you know that you can book an appointment up to two weeks in advance on-line? Visit www…'

Leo didn't make many telephone calls. He had been brought up when the telephone, like chicken, was a comparative luxury and calls were expensive. He put the phone down. He would do as suggested and call another time.

'Switchboard is very busy today. Please hold and your call will be answered as soon as one of our receptionists becomes available. You are currently number twenty-one in the queue…'

Leo put the phone down again, perhaps a little more forcefully than strictly necessary. He wondered how they knew that he was twenty-first in the queue. He noticed that there had been a slight pause or hesitation before the number was spoken, as if someone were counting before saying the number. If so, he or she had to be very quick.

He tried again the next day, with a similar result. It was true that it was cold and rainy, just the weather for coughs and colds, so perhaps it was true that the surgery was abnormally busy. On a fourth attempt, he resolved to wait.

After more than fifteen minutes of a recording of *Greensleeves* that seemed to have been made under water, interspersed with repetitions of the message informing him of his progress up the queue, there was a kind of clattering noise and a lady, who sounded slightly irritated, answered.

'Surgery,' she said.

'Hello, I'm calling about a wheelchair,' said Leo.

'Name?'

Leo gave it.

'How are you spelling that?'

Leo spelt it, not without slight difficulty. He wasn't used to it.

'Date of birth?'

He gave it.

'First line of your address?'

Leo gave the whole of it.

'I only need the first line.'

He could hear some tapping of the keys of a computer, which then stopped. The lady went silent, and he could hear a background hum of conversation and the tap-tap of other computer keyboards. Leo asked whether the lady was still there.

'Of course.'

'Well…' said Leo.

'What is it that you want?' asked the lady.

'As I said, I need a wheelchair. You see, I can't get around…'

'Let me stop you there. To get a wheelchair, you'll have to see the doctor.'

'How do I do that?'

'You make an appointment, of course.'

'Can I make one then?'

'They're fully booked for the next two weeks.'

'Well, can I have one after that, then?'

'We don't make appointments more than two weeks in advance.'

'What can I do, then?'

'You have two choices. You can phone every morning early to make an appointment for two weeks' time, or you can come down to the surgery. There are a few slots every day for people without appointments.'

'But I can't get down to the surgery, I've got this leg in plaster.'

'There's nothing else I can do.'

'Can't the doctor come out to see me?'

The receptionist was scandalised: Oliver Twist had asked

for more.

'The doctors don't make home visits any more, they haven't for years. It's not an efficient use of their time.'

'What am I to do, then?'

'You could go back to the hospital. You could call hospital transport.'

'But the hospital says I have to speak to my doctor.'

'Then you'll have to come to the surgery.'

'But I can't.'

'Surely you know someone who could bring you?'

Leo thought for a moment.

'I'm not sure,' he said.

'I've got a lot of other callers on the line. I can't help you any more, I'm afraid.'

The line went dead. Leo looked at the receiver and shook it gently as if there might have been a loose connection to account for the silence.

'Hello?' he said. 'Hello?'

There was no answer, and then a meaningless noise emerged from it, and he replaced the receiver.

He started to think. First, he would have to find someone to take him to the doctors. Mrs Phillips next door had a son who visited her sometimes and had a smart car. Perhaps he would take him. Leo had never spoken to him much, in fact hardly knew him even by sight, but Mrs Phillips was always saying that he was a good lad (although more than forty), do anything for anybody, he would. The problem was that his visits to his mother were sporadic and unreliable, as if he visited only when passing in any case. Even Mrs Phillips didn't know when he was visiting next. He might come, in fact he probably would, when the doctors' surgery was closed. Still, Leo couldn't think of anyone else. Next time Mrs Phillips brought his 'bit of shopping', he asked her whether her Jason could take him to the surgery. She said that he probably would, if asked, but couldn't say when his next visit was likely to be. It depended on his work; he was very busy because he had an important job.

Luckily, Jason visited one morning the following week. He agreed to take Leo to the doctors', although it didn't please him particularly to do so. He had to park his car outside Leo's house, which obstructed the traffic and caused angry drivers to make faces, or even shake their fists, at him. A couple of them shouted obscenities.

'You f...... blind or something?' shouted an exceptionally angry man, rolling down his window to shout at him as he passed. 'Can't you see them double yellow lines?'

'And can't you f...... see that I'm trying to help a cripple?' shouted back Jason, more to relieve his feelings than in the hope that the driver of the passing car, which had accelerated past the obstruction, would hear.

It was difficult to manoeuvre Leo into the car. His plaster cast was large and heavy and reached almost to his hip, and it was as if he had to learn to stand on it, like a baby taking its first steps. He was clumsy, and Jason, who had never really wanted the task of taking him to the doctors', grew impatient with him and treated him as if he were an awkward-shaped parcel that had to be squeezed, trying various angles, into a space only just large enough for it. Once in, of course, it would be just as difficult to get it out again.

'Perhaps they'll lend you a wheelchair down the surgery to

help me into the building,' said Leo, lying across the back seat.

That was a good idea. Jason pulled up at the surgery, in a little bay near the entrance marked 'Drop off only. No waiting. Overstayers will be clamped. Release fee £150.' The sign was posted by Parking Solutions Ltd., whose mission statement was 'Keeping your space free.'

Jason left Leo in the car and went into the building, whose doors slid obligingly open for him as he approached them. There was quite a queue of people inside, waiting to speak to the receptionists. He joined it.

Jason grew irritated. No one ahead of him appeared to know what he wanted or was capable of saying it at less than essay length. All of them were old except for a young mother whose toddler started running off and screamed whenever she dragged him back by his arm. The receptionists had to answer their telephones as well; it seemed that their conversations with callers took hours.

Eventually he reached the counter. The receptionist had a badge pinned to her chemise: *We're here to help.*

'Yes?' said the receptionist.

'I've come to ask whether you can lend me a wheelchair. I've got a man outside with a broken leg.'

'Name?'

'His or mine?'

'Both.'

Jason gave Leo's name and his own. The receptionist seemed to attack the keyboard of her computer angrily, as if it had just misbehaved. Her eyes roamed the screen in front of her, making them look like those of a sheep.

'How are you spelling your name?' she asked. 'I can't find

you.'

'I'm not registered here,' said Jason.

'Why didn't you say? I've wasted my time.'

'Anyway, I need a wheelchair for Mr Smith.'

'We can't lend one to someone who's not registered here.'

'Mr Smith is registered here.'

'Yes, but you're not, and you're the one we'd be lending it to. How do we know you're not making it up? You might run off with it. Wheelchairs are expensive, you know.'

'He's outside in the car. You can come and see for yourself.'

'I can't possibly leave the desk. Look at all the people in the line behind you. You're not the only person here. Besides, I'm not allowed to go out to a patient. I'm not qualified, and the insurance doesn't cover it.'

'I'll have to try to bring him in, then.'

'Looks like it.'

Jason returned to the car. A man in a uniform had just finished placing a clamp on the front wheel. Across the clamp was a yellow steel notice saying, 'Do not attempt to remove'.

'I've got a man with a broken leg in there,' said Jason to the man.

'That's not my problem,' said the man in the uniform. 'You was here longer than five minutes, and five minutes is the maximum. It says so on the notice.' He pointed to the notice.

'I was trying to get a wheelchair to take him into the surgery,' said Jason, making movements with his head to indicate Leo and then the surgery.

'The rules is the rules, mate, I don't make them.'

'Couldn't you see that he was waiting to be taken inside?'

'I'm only doing my job. My job is to clamp vehicles that

stop here for more than five minutes. You stopped here for more than five minutes.'

'Well, now you know why we were here, can't you remove the clamp?'

'It's more than my job's worth to do that. Besides, I can't.'

'Why not?'

'Because they don't give me the equipment. Once the clamp's on, it's on. The only way to get it off is to call the company. You can try explaining to them. The number to call's on the notice.' The man in uniform walked off.

There was nothing for it but for Jason to call the company.

'Thank you for calling Parking Solutions Limited. All our operators are busy at the moment, but your call will be answered as soon as one becomes available. Please note that for training and security purposes, your call may be recorded to help us give you a better service. Thank you for your patience.'

Then came an extract of *Eine kleine Nachtmusik*, over and over again. Jason turned on Leo, having opened the door to the back seat on which he was lying.

'Couldn't you have told that bastard why we were here?' he asked.

'I tried to, but he wouldn't listen'

Eine kleine Nachtmusik stopped.

'Parking Solutions Limited, how may I help you?'

'You've clamped my car,' said Jason.

'Address?'

'The point is, you had no right to do it. I was trying to get a wheelchair to take a man with a broken leg into a doctor's surgery.'

'I'm afraid I can't discuss that. I'm here only to take your location and payment.'

'But that's outrageous…'

'You can appeal in writing or online after you've made the payment. The notice tells you how.'

'And what if I refuse?'

'Your car will be towed away after two hours and a charge for towing and release applies.'

There seemed to be no way out. Jason said he would pay but he would contact his Member of Parliament.

'Card number?' 'Name as it appears on card?' 'Expiry date?' 'Security number, the three digits on the back of the card?'

'When will they come to remove the clamp?' asked Jason.

'I can't give you a time. They're very busy today. Between two and three hours.'

'That shows how necessary it is for there to be no cars parked here, doesn't it?'

'There's no need to be like that. I'm only doing my job.'

She rang off. Jason thought he might as well try to take Leo into the surgery.

It took a long time. Leo could manage only one step at a time, was very unsteady and uncertain, and had to pause often to rest. Jason, who kept looking irritably at his watch as a matter of principle, had to keep near him, supporting him by the elbow to give him the confidence to continue.

At length, they reached the reception counter. Leo was obviously exhausted by the effort.

'Yes?' said the receptionist, this time a different one who had glitter on the plastic wings of her spectacles.

'We've come about a wheelchair for Mr Smith,' said Jason, taking the lead.

'You'll have to see a doctor about that.'

'Yes, he wants to see one.'

'You can't today, it's emergencies only. All the doctors are in their monthly audit meeting.'

'What's that?' asked Leo.

The receptionist looked at him as if he were a boy who had failed to revise properly for a school exam.

'It's a requirement of the government's *Reflective Practice Programme*, the RPP. You must have heard of it, it was on the news months ago.'

'No,' said Leo.

'Every month the doctors set aside a session so that they can reflect on what they're doing, to see what's wrong and how they can correct it.'

'So what does Mr Smith do?' interjected Jason.

'He can come back tomorrow. I can't guarantee he'll be seen, though.'

'But how can he come back? He has no transport.' Jason was beginning to shout.

'There's no need to raise your voice.'

Just then, a doctor emerged from one of the rooms on the ground floor.

'What's going on?' he asked. He knew from experience when tempers were rising.

'This man needs a wheelchair,' said Jason, stepping forward a little belligerently. 'It's difficult for him to get here and she's saying he can't see a doctor.' Jason indicated the receptionist with his head.

The doctor was a kindly man, not far off retirement.

'Let's have a look at you,' he said to Leo.

'I broke my leg in four places,' said Leo, not without pride, as if it had been an achievement.

'You'll be in plaster for some time, then,' said the doctor.

'Yes, and the surgeon said he wasn't sure if it'll heal completely. He said I might not be able to walk normal again. He said that even if I did, I could get arthuritis later. So you see, I need a wheelchair.' Then he added irrelevantly, 'I was a postman.'

The doctor turned to the receptionist, who had been listening to the conversation irritably, even indignantly, for it undermined her authority to deny the patient a consultation. This man was plainly jumping the queue. Just because he couldn't walk very well and the doctor happened to meet him, he thought he could beat the system. Many of the patients were like that, mind you, trying to get something to which they were not entitled. Her job was not an easy one.

'Could you call up his notes on the computer?' the doctor asked her.

'Yes, doctor,' said the receptionist. 'Name?' she asked, turning to Leo. 'Date of birth?' 'First line of the address?'

'There you are,' she said to the doctor, barely disguising her disapproval. The doctor went behind the desk to look at the screen.

'Nasty fracture,' he said. 'Clearly you'll need a wheelchair.'

Leo smiled. 'Thank you, doctor. Can I have one, then?'

'Unfortunately,' said the doctor, 'it's not entirely up to me. If it were, you'd have one straight away, of course. But it's not entirely up to me, I'll have to ask the Wheelchair Coordinator.

She covers the whole area. She'll come to your house and assess your needs.'

'But I need a wheelchair,' said Leo. 'You said so yourself.'

'Yes, I know, but that's the system. There's a shortage of wheelchairs, and so they have to be prioritised. It's up to her to decide how urgent it is.'

'When will she come?'

'I know that she's very busy at the moment. She was on maternity leave until recently, and there's a backlog. I'll see what I can do. Of course, I can't promise anything. I think it'll be about a fortnight.'

'That's a long time,' said Leo. 'Can't she come no quicker than that?'

'As I said, I'll try,' said the doctor. 'Of course, there's another solution.'

'What's that?'

'You could buy a wheelchair yourself. I think you can get one for about three hundred pounds, though I'm not sure. Or you could rent one.'

Leo had very few savings, for he had never earned much more than his living expenses, and his pension was small. Besides, he had paid his taxes and the idea of paying for what he was entitled to struck him as unjust.

'If I paid my taxes, why should I have to buy a wheelchair as well?'

'It's not my fault, I'm afraid,' said the doctor. 'That's just how things are.'

'I'll have to wait then,' said Leo.

'I'll get on to the Wheelchair Coordinator straight away,' said the doctor. 'I'll tell her you're a priority.' So saying, he turned to rejoin the audit meeting.

When finally his car was unclamped (sooner than expected), Jason returned Leo home. He was cross, but also a little proud to have been so good a Samaritan. He never wanted to see Leo again.

Leo now had to wait for the Wheelchair Coordinator. He had no means of communicating with her, nor did he know when she would come, but it hardly mattered since he was unable to go anywhere and was always at home. They also serve who only sit and wait.

One day, Leo was in his tiny bathroom when there was a loud and perfunctory rap on his door. It gave him a start.

'Coming,' he shouted, but it was a struggle for him to get to the front door.

By the time he reached and opened it, whoever had called was gone. But there was a little card that had been pushed through the letterbox and that Leo stooped painfully to pick up. It said, 'I am sorry you were out when I called, but I will call again soon.' It was signed (printed) *Your Wheelchair Coordinator*, who had naturally concluded from the absence of reply to her call that Leo was out and therefore that his need for a wheelchair was not really urgent. Like almost everyone else, he could be placed at the bottom of the waiting list.

It was two weeks before she called again. She was a woman in her early forties but reluctant to admit to herself that she was no longer in her twenties. Her hair cascaded from her head in unnatural strands of various shades of brown and gold. She was dressed brightly and vividly made up.

After introducing herself and asking whether she could come inside, she asked Leo what she should call him.

'What do you mean?' asked Leo, slightly bemused.

'I mean, do you want to be Leopold, or Leo for short, or Mr Smith?' she said, laughing. 'We always ask.'

'I... I don't know.'

'I'll call you Leo, then, it's friendlier, isn't it?'

She sat down and watched Leo struggling to do likewise.

'Mr Smith would sound so formal, wouldn't it? Like there was a difference between us.'

'Well, there is, isn't there?'

'You mean your leg? Of course. I've heard you've had a nasty break, and that's why you would like a wheelchair.'

'Yes, I can't get around much. I have to hobble, and I've been told not to put any weight on my leg.'

'It has to have a chance to heal.'

'That's what they say.'

'No where would you go in your wheelchair, if you had one?'

'Well, out and about, to the shops, things like that. Not far.'

'You've got someone who does your shopping already?'

Leo noticed that she had a clipboard and was jotting down his answers.

'Yes, her next door, but I don't like to ask.'

The Wheelchair Coordinator ticked a paper on her clipboard and wrote a few words.

'So you really want a wheelchair just to get out now and again?'

'It'd be useful. I need some fresh air sometimes.'

'I can understand that,' said the Wheelchair Coordinator, looking round Leo's front room, which was small, dark and cheaply furnished in the ugly style of the 1940s. 'Being stuck indoors all the time.' She wrote something else down. Then she said, 'I think there's a step up from the pavement to your front door, isn't there?'

'Yes,' said Leo. 'It's difficult for me now.'

The Wheelchair Coordinator stood up, went over to the front door, opened it and looked down.

'Very difficult for a wheelchair,' she said sorrowfully, 'especially if you're on your own. It'd be difficult to get down to the pavement and up again.'

'I could lever it,' said Leo. 'You know, tip it backwards on its wheels and steer it.'

'I wouldn't advise that. You'd be surprised how many accidents happen that way. You've had enough accidents for the time being, haven't you?'

'You could put a ramp from the door to the pavement.'

The Wheelchair Coordinator steeped out of the front door and had a look. She returned shaking her head.

'That wouldn't work,' she said. 'Any ramp would lead straight out on to the road. It would be very dangerous.'

She patted Leo lightly on the shoulder.

'You'll hear from me soon,' she said, just as she departed.

Two weeks later, a brown envelope dropped through the letterbox. In it was a white document headed *National Wheelchair Distribution Agency*, with a picture of a wheel dragging a flag with the words *Bringing mobility to the injured* under it:

I am sorry to inform you that your application for a wheelchair has

not been accepted.

Then came a list of pre-printed reasons, two of which were ticked:

Not essential for daily living

Would put the life of the applicant and/or others at risk

The document finished 'If you disagree with this decision and wish to appeal it, you have 14 working days from the date of this letter to do so. Call 0330 001299 for the Wheelchair Appeal Helpline.'

The letter was dated three weeks earlier.

THE WAR OF THE ROSES

Ever since the Roses moved in next door, they had been nothing but trouble. Mr Rose was a retired businessman of some kind who soon let it be known that, by moving there, he was not involuntarily accepting much less luxury and grandeur than that to which he was accustomed or indeed could still afford, but rather that, thinking of his old age, he had decided that somewhere smaller and more manageable would be advisable — though the house was still large enough for a family with several children.

Mrs Rose, by contrast, gave the immediate impression of madness but without evoking the sympathy that affliction would normally evoke. On the contrary, her prominent staring eyes, staccato speech (which was mainly monosyllabic), and unpredictable gesticulations gave rise more to fear, as if she were about to commit an act of violence with a concealed knife. She was startled if anyone said 'Good morning' to her, as if it were an intrusion on her privacy or contained a concealed meaning, and there was always a long pause before she would respond.

No sooner had they moved in than the Roses erected

scaffolding around the house adjoining that of the Finches, it being necessary for them to demonstrate that the house was not up to their own standard. The Finches were a professional couple, he being a barrister of uncertain practice, a keen follower of, and loser by, the turf, she a high-flying banker who carried over banking principles into daily life. She thought it her duty to bargain in department stores, for example, on the grounds that if everyone did so, prices would fall. She often triumphed in her endeavour, obtaining goods at well below the price that everyone else, too timid to follow suit, paid.

It was clear from the start that the Roses and the Finches were ill-assorted. Both couples felt themselves the superior of the other, and just as one Napoleon in a psychiatric ward can see through the pretensions of another, so the Roses and Finches saw through the pretensions of their new neighbours. Each thought that they had more money, and moreover that the provenance of their money was superior, ethically and socially. But they also thought that open rivalry was beneath them: one competes only with equals, or near equals.

Mr Rose soon revealed himself to be a perpetual tinkerer on a large scale. He thought he was a better builder, carpenter, plasterer, plumber, electrician and decorator than any mere professional, who besides their incompetence were usually dishonest into the bargain. He evidently had some blueprint in his mind, a kind of platonic ideal of his own house, to which he was always approximating but never reaching. No sooner had the paint of his colour scheme dried, for example, than he brought out his blowtorch to burn it off so that he could start again. The smell of burnt paint lingered permanently in his house, along with that of poured cements, various types of glue, and other such materials. It was the equivalent of incense in oriental temples.

Two months after their arrival, the Roses sought permission from the council to extend their property at its rear. Though the house was far too large for the needs of two people, Mr Rose insisted that it was not large enough for him and his wife, who felt cramped by it, accustomed as they were to more and larger rooms. Their plan was grandiose: it would nearly have doubled the size of their house and spread it well into the back garden, blocking the light of the Finches for several hours a day. Naturally, when asked whether they had any objections, the Finches objected vigorously, Mrs Finch particularly. The council knew instinctively that approval would give them more trouble than refusal, and so they refused.

Of course, Mr Rose appealed, but his appeal only strengthened Mrs Finch's resolve to thwart him. She had not only her own interests at heart, she said, but those of the whole area in which they lived, which would be disfigured by Mr Rose's proposals. Once again, she triumphed over him.

Mr Rose was not the kind of man to accept defeat without retaliation. Rancour with him was no passing mood but a permanent state, to be nursed by memory and increased by reflection. He harboured a resentment against his neighbours all the greater because he saw Mr Finch as a wastrel and a parasite, going off for a day at the races when, at his age, he should have been working. Who did he think he was to behave like a degenerate aristocrat? Mr Rose was of humble stock who had raised himself by his own exertions. Whenever he crossed the path of one of his neighbours, he refused from now on to pass the time of day with them, even as perfunctorily as he had done before they opposed his plans for his house. As for Mrs Rose, she seemed to be in a different world altogether, with her staring eyes and intermittent gesticulations.

Occasionally the Finches had rows, usually about Mr Finch's fecklessness after a debauch on what Mr Finch called the *gee-gees*. Generally, Mrs Finch accepted her husband whole, faults and all (he was a charmer), but occasionally it got too much for her, and if she had had a particularly bad or difficult day she would explode at him like a grenade. Then she had a loud and penetrating voice, and though the walls of the house were usually thick enough to blot the sound out, the Roses could, by straining their ears, hear her.

One day, there was a particularly loud quarrel between the Finches. Mr Finch, apparently, had blown several thousand at the races and though this represented only a small fraction of Mrs Finch's annual bonus, she was understandably furious.

'If you go on like that,' she shouted, 'you'll ruin us.'

His replies to a string of such reproaches, of lower vocal timbre, could not be made out next door. There was a slamming of doors and banging of furniture. Mr Rose called the police.

'There's violence next door,' he said. 'I think a murder might be about to be committed.'

By the time the police arrived, their quarrel was over, and the Finches had gone to bed. The loud knocking on the door and repeated ringing on the bell startled them. When Mr Finch, in pyjamas and dressing gown opened the door, he was confronted by two policemen in stab vests, and with truncheons, gas canisters and handcuffs dangling from their belts, like decorations on a prison warder's Christmas tree.

'We've been informed of a disturbance here,' said one of them.

'Who told you that?' asked Mr Finch, though he could very well guess.

'We can't tell you that. What's been going on here?'

'What's been going on? Nothing's been going on, as you put it.'

'We've had reports of a violent dispute.'

'Nonsense.'

'Can we have a look around?'

'What do you expect to find, a body?'

'It has been known,' said the second policeman.

'Do you have a warrant?' said Mr Finch with the petulance of the weak.

'We don't need one if we have reasonable grounds.'

One of the policemen already had his foot over the threshold.

'What's going on down there?' asked a commanding woman's voice from upstairs.

'It's the police, darling,' called up Mr Finch.

'Whatever for?'

'They say there's been a disturbance here.'

'Fiddlesticks.'

Mrs Finch now appeared at the head of the stairs in a cream satin nightgown.

'What are you doing here?' she asked the police imperiously.

'We've heard of a disturbance in this house, madam.'

'Well, you've heard wrong, haven't you, you're not wanted or needed here.'

The two policemen looked at each other. Their confidence had evaporated. Evidently the quarrellers were uninjured, and there was no need to search for bodies in the dining room.

'Please go,' said Mrs Finch.

'We have to investigate reports of domestics,' said the first policeman, almost apologetically. 'I'm sure you'll understand. Most murders start as domestics.'

'But most domestics, as you call them, don't end in murder,' said Mrs Finch firmly. She was a financial analyst. 'Besides, there hasn't even been a domestic in the first place.'

'All right, madam,' said the second policeman. 'We're leaving. Just quarrel a bit quieter next time.' With this barb, he saved the honour of the police.

After they had gone, Mrs Finch turned to her husband, 'Why did you let them in?'

'They insisted…'

'You should've shut the door in their faces. They had no right to enter. You're a lawyer, after all…'

'It must have been the Roses who called them,' said Mr Finch, diverting attention from his weakness.

'Of course it must've been.' Mrs Finch often reproached her husband for saying the obvious. 'Who else could it have been?'

Mr Rose's call to the police was his declaration of war or opening shot in that war. He was not the kind of man to forget, much less to forgive, a slight or an insult, which is how he interpreted opposition to his plans. He hadn't succeeded in business by being nice, besides which malignity was more interesting.

One of the trees in the Finches' garden overhung the fence between them. On a fine day, Mr Rose took out his ladder and his chainsaw and lopped the branches. He wielded the saw like a swordsman in a mediaeval battle. He leaned over the fence and cut, or hacked, branches well on the Finches' side. When he finished, the tree looked as forlorn as a dog with mange. Branches, twigs and foliage had fallen into the Finches' garden.

The Finches were furious — especially Mrs Finch, who enjoyed being furious. She thought, though, that it would be best to send her husband to complain. All their marriage she had been trying to put some backbone into him, at the same time knowing it to be impossible and not really wanting it. In fact, it was she who had pushed him into being a barrister, a profession unsuitable for him. Left to himself, he would have frittered all his time away rather than most of it.

He rang the Roses' bell. It was Mrs Rose who opened the door. Her eyes stared unblinkingly. Mr Finch was disconcerted.

'Er…' he said by way of explanation of his visit.

By a supreme intellectual effort, Mrs Rose managed to ask him what he wanted.

'The tree…' said Mr Finch. 'You've cut its branches on our side.'

'*I* didn't,' said Mrs Rose.

'I don't mean you personally,' said Mr Finch. 'I mean you as a household.'

'You mean my husband?'

'Yes, there's no one else.'

'Well, don't go around accusing people, then.'

'I didn't accuse people. I was merely saying that you've cut branches on our side of the fence which you had no right to do.'

'That's an accusation.'

'If so, it's justified. You — you or your husband, it doesn't matter which — cut branches on our side of the fence.'

'What if it had been a tree surgeon?'

'That's quibbling. One or other of you must've done it or given orders for it to be done.'

'You'll have to speak to my husband.'

'All right, I'll speak to him. Where is he?'

'Out.'

Mr Finch didn't believe it, but there was nothing more he could do. Mrs Rose slammed the door shut. Mr Finch returned home and reported to his wife. She was unimpressed by his efforts and marched round herself to the Roses. She not only rang the bell but knocked vigorously on the door. It was Mr Rose who answered it.

'I should like a word with you,' she said.

'It's not convenient at the moment,' said Mr Rose.

'I don't care.' She insinuated herself into the hallway.

'You're trespassing, I could have you for that.'

'Don't be ridiculous. You invited me in.'

'I didn't.'

'It's only your word against mine. You've no witnesses.'

'My wife.'

'I don't think she'd make a very good witness.'

'And what exactly do you mean by that?'

'I haven't come to discuss your wife's illness. I want to talk to you about the tree that you've cut.'

'Pruned,' said Mr Rose.

'Decimated,' said Mrs Finch.

'It was about time. The branches were out of control.'

'That's not true, but even if it were, it would have been our problem. You could've asked.'

'They were blocking our light.'

'It's not true. You're making it up.'

'How do you know? How *could* you know? You've never been on our side of the fence, in our garden.'

'I don't need to have been to know that what you're saying is ridiculous.'

'You can't say that.'

'I just have.'

'That tree was a nuisance.'

'It was doing no harm.'

'There were pigeons in it all the time.'

'And so?'

'They made a constant mess. They took all the food for the other birds from our bird table.'

'You're not going to apologise?'

'There's nothing to apologise for.'

'We'll see about that.'

When she returned home, Mr Finch asked her how she had got on. She didn't reply but marched out into the back garden, her husband following. She pointed to the fallen branches and foliage.

'Throw them over the fence,' she said to Mr Finch.

In addition to his other qualities, Mr Finch was physically lazy. He always exerted himself as little as possible. He looked at the scattered branches.

'Some of them are very heavy,' he said. He also disliked getting his hands dirty.

'Not *that* heavy,' said his wife. 'Just chuck'em over.'

'I've got my jacket on.'

'Take it off.'

There was no escape, and Mr Finch began to throw the branches over the fence. His pale face glistened with the effort.

'Is that enough?' he asked.

'All,' said his wife. 'I don't see why we should keep any.'

As he was coming to the end of the task, they heard a voice from the other side of the fence.

'What the hell do you think you're doing?'

'We're returning your rubbish to you,' said Mrs Finch.

'It's not mine, it's yours. They're branches from your side of the tree.'

'You made the mess, you clear it up.'

There was a brief silence from the other side. Then Mr Rose returned to the attack.

'Look, you've damaged the fence by throwing things over it.'

The fence was of wooden slats, and it was true that there was now a little triangle of missing wood from the top of one of them.

'That's been there a long time,' said Mrs Finch.

'No it hasn't, you've just done it.'

'Look,' said Mrs Finch. 'You can see it's weathered where it's broken. It's not the same colour at all, it's much darker.'

'I don't agree.'

'It's not a matter of opinion, it's a matter of fact. Anyway, whether new or old, it's up to you to repair it. It's your fence, on your land.' And she threw a small branch with a few leaves attached back over it.

There was the simulacrum of a truce for a day or two, or so it seemed. Then a letter arrived for the Finches from the Roses' lawyers. According to the letter, the fence between the gardens was badly placed, usurping a four-inch strip of the Roses' land. The Roses would therefore be obliged if the Finches would remove the fence and put it in its proper place.

'We're not going to move the fence just because of a lawyer's letter,' said Mrs Finch. 'We'll have to get a surveyor.'

The surveyor was costly and dilatory. A slightly more menacing letter arrived from the Roses' lawyer. Unfortunately for the Finches, moreover, the surveyor found that the Roses were correct: the fence did usurp some of their land, albeit only three, not four, inches of it. They would have to move it. While the work was being done, Mr Rose smirked whenever he crossed Mrs Finch's path.

Mrs Finch was not accustomed to defeat, quite the contrary, and revenge would be a kind of victory. It did not take her long to find a way.

They lived in what was called a conservation area, that is to say an area of architectural merit or historical interest (in the opinion of the local council), in which the owners of the houses were required to consult a council bureaucrat before making any alterations to their properties. This Mr Rose had failed to do before he embarked on his various works, and the mauve that he painted his front door was particularly shocking.

Mrs Finch wrote to the council as one who was performing her public duty. She said that she thought the area ought to be preserved for future generations. She listed the ways in which Mr Rose's alterations had, inadvertently she was sure, violated the style and spirit of the original buildings.

Victorians, she said, would never have painted their front doors mauve. There was no other front door remotely like it in the street, in which stood a Gothic revival church. It should surely be painted a more subdued colour in keeping with the area.

Then there were the windows on the first floor. Originally, they had been — as in the Finches' own house — of the sash variety, but Mr Rose had replaced them by a cheaper modern variety, also out of keeping with the area.

There was also a small wall in the front garden that Mr Rose had rebuilt using modern bricks, such that it looked like an angry scar. He had failed to use appropriate bricks: either recuperated Victorian ones, or at least bricks in the Victorian style, either of which were easily available. The result was an eyesore.

Finally, though Mrs Finch had not visited Mr Rose's house, the fact that he had, to her certain knowledge, undertaken extensive interior alterations and had shown no respect for the original features of the exterior, made it likely that he had altered the original fabric of the interior, destroying its Victorian qualities. Moreover, she *had* been able to see through the windows of the ground floor, and it was clear that the original plasterwork, for example of the cornices, was no more. This was vandalism in the guise of refurbishment.

A couple of weeks later, the Roses received a visit from the council's employee in charge of conservation. He was an officious little man who delighted in disapproval. He looked at things from a distance and then squinted at them close up. He made sounds that sounded like 'Tut, tut!' as he worked, and shook his head slightly as he made them. He asked Mr Rose when he had made the alterations — Mrs Rose accompanied her husband, but he disregarded her entirely.

'Did you contact the Conservation Department before making them?' he asked, knowing the answer so well that his question was more accusation than interrogative.

'Why should I?' said Mr Rose. 'It's my house.'

'It's your house, but it's in a conservation area. That means that any substantial alterations to structure or appearance must be approved in advance. You must have been told that when you bought it.'

Mr Rose denied it and found the rule outrageous in any case. The house was his property to do what he liked with.

'Not in a conservation area, your solicitor must have apprised you of it.'

'He didn't.'

'Well, you should take it up with him. My job is only to enforce the rules.' He looked at the list he had made of Mr Rose's offences against conservation. 'First you'll have to paint your front door another colour.' He produced a chart illustrating permitted colours.

'My wife and I like it as it is, don't we Rose?' Mrs Rose's first name was Rosemary, so that in the days when the Roses, before her illness, frequented people, she was known as Rose-Rose.

'Yes,' she said, looking at the conservation officer with her strange, disconcerting, unblinking stare.

'I'm afraid that's beside the point,' said the officious little man drawing himself up to his full height and puffing out his chest. 'We do, of course, allow minor variations in choice of colour — the chart is only a guide — but you mustn't stray too far from it.'

'This is ridiculous!' exclaimed Mr Rose. 'It's a dictatorship.'

'It's the law, but you can appeal. You have twenty-eight days from notice in which to do so.'

'This is absurd,' said Mr Rose. 'Look at the monstrosities you give permission to build, and you object to the colour of my front door!'

'That's not my department. The Planning and Conservation Departments are completely separate. We have different remits.'

Mr Rose spluttered rather than spoke.

'And the windows,' said the conservation officer. 'They will have to be replaced by sash windows in the original style. You can have them made.'

'But that will cost a fortune.'

'I'm afraid that's not my affair.' He looked round the room in which they were now sitting. 'And all the plaster cornices and ceiling will have to be restored. We'll send you a schedule of the works to be done as soon as possible.' He got up to go.

'It's the Finches next door, isn't it, who've put you up to all this, isn't it?' Mr Rose said.

'I can't discuss that. In any case, no matter the source of our information, the rules are the rules. It's irrelevant.'

'Not to us, it isn't,' said Mr Rose.

After the official had gone, Mr Rose said to his wife, 'It's them, of course, it's them. Did you hear how he avoided the question? Just because we asked them to return what we had a right to anyway.'

Mrs Rose grimaced and gesticulated; she had caught her hatred of their neighbours from her husband, like a disease.

A letter from the Conservation Department (situated in the council's head offices, a concrete office block due for demolition twenty-eight years after its construction, despite the protests of a few who said that it was a fine example of its genre, with its 'stark and honest' geometry and flat leaking roof) arrived two weeks later. It demanded the restoration of the house within a period of six months and added that there would be no grant for this work because it was necessitated by unauthorised changes made by the owners. At further expense, Mr Rose consulted a lawyer who told him that he could object to the demand but would probably lose any case.

Mr Rose turned his thoughts to revenge, a subject always close to his heart.

The Finches had a cat of some rare, exotic and expensive breed. Of felines it was the most feline: that is to say, elegant, sly and underhand. It was an enthusiastic hunter of birds and did great slaughter among them, especially of the smaller and prettier type. It would bite their heads off and leave their divided cadavers on the Roses' garden terrace, as if it had been instructed to. There would be feathers and blood, some of the feathers sticking to the stone when the blood dried. The cat's name was Slinky, which at least was appropriate.

Mr Rose tackled Mrs Finch on the cat question one day as she got into her car.

'Your cat is killing birds in our garden,' he said.

'How do you know it's Slinky?'

'It leaves dead birds on the terrace. It's upsetting my wife.'

'That could be anybody's cat, there are plenty round here. To say nothing of weasels.' Mrs Finch was pleased with the ingenuity of her reply.

'It's obvious it's your cat. I've seen it in our garden. You ought to control it.'

Mrs Finch let loose a snort of derision.

'Have you ever tried to control a cat?' she asked, who loved Slinky more than anyone in the world.

'You'll have to keep it indoors,' said Mr Rose.

'You can't tell me what I must and mustn't do.'

'No, you get the Conservation Department to do it for you.'

'I don't know what you mean.'

'I think you do.'

'I don't.'

'We ought to protect garden birds.'

Mrs Finch slammed the door of her car and drove off.

Mr Rose was secretly pleased that she had been unreasonable and unbending — as he had expected her to be. It gave him his justification for his next step, into which he had already done some research.

First, he put out some milk for Slinky. Superficially he may have been a superior creature, thought Mr Rose, but airs and graces notwithstanding it was still only a cat, and no cat could resist milk. He was right: Slinky lapped it up.

Mr Rose next bought some antifreeze, not in the local garage where he might be recognised, but at a large station where he would not be remembered. Cats like antifreeze, and it kills them.

But first he habituated Slinky to his saucer of milk in the mornings, telling his wife that she must put it out at the same time every day. It was not long before Slinky came to demand his milk, as if of right. It was now time to poison him.

'Today's the day,' thought Mr Rose, as he poured some

antifreeze into the milk that his wife was to put down for Slinky. He told his wife to make sure that Slinky returned home after his daily milk, which Slinky did. He would be ill in half an hour.

Everything went according to plan. Half an hour after his return from the Roses' garden, Slinky began to vomit copiously and be unsteady on his feet. Mrs Finch was away at work, and Mr Finch was studying the form of today's races in a room whose French windows gave on to the back garden. He noticed Slinky stagger as if drunk, fall over on his side and struggle unsteadily on to his legs, only to fall again. He didn't want to be distracted from his studies, so he thought that perhaps cats were like that from time to time. It was a passing phase, and he resumed his perusal of the *Sporting Times*: Jahan's Boy was a good bet for the 2.30 at Catterick. The odds were long, but not absurdly so, and the going would suit him. He put the paper down preparatory to making his bet by telephone and glanced out of the French windows again. Slinky was lying motionless on the ground, apart from some intermittent gasps for air, and some foam was emerging from his mouth and nostrils. Mr Finch did what was natural for him in these circumstances and phoned his wife, having briefly examined Slinky without touching him. Mr Finch was a fastidious man who did not like dirt of any kind.

Mrs Finch was in a meeting, so she spoke in a low but nevertheless irritated voice.

'I can't speak for long,' she said. Negotiations were at a critical stage.

'Slinky's very ill,' said Mr Finch. 'I think he's dying.'

'Take him to the vet, then,' said Mrs Finch. Even when

upset she was practical — perhaps more so than ever.

Mr Finch had to overcome his distaste in order to take the prostrate Slinky in his arms. The creature was soft and warm but dead. It was too late for the vet to do anything, but nevertheless Mr Finch did what his wife said, even if useless. It was best that way.

There was not much of a wait at the vet's: there was only a sick rabbit and a puppy for injection before him.

'I think my cat's dead,' he said as he entered the vet's consulting room and laid Slinky on the examination table. He described Slinky's symptoms before his demise.

The vet bent low over Slinky and sniffed a few times.

'Ethylene glycol,' he said.

'What?' said Mr Finch.

'Ethylene glycol. Antifreeze. It's a common agent that kills cats. They like it because it tastes sweet to them, but it kills them.'

'You mean, people poison cats with antifreeze?'

'Mostly it's accidental. People leave it around or spill it, and the cats lap it up.'

'It must've been our neighbour. He hated Slinky.'

As he left the vet's office, the receptionist gave him a pamphlet, *When Your Pet Dies*. It contained the address of the pet crematorium, as well as that of a grief counsellor. Mr Finch took Slinky home.

When Mrs Finch returned from work, they buried Slinky in the flowerbed as near the fence as possible. It was now dark, so the burial had the air of furtiveness about it, more like an exhumation than an interment.

'We'll have a headstone made,' said Mrs Finch. 'Slinky,

cruelly poisoned by the neighbours.'

She called the police. She was morally sure of the Roses' guilt. It was difficult to interest the police, the victim being only a cat, and it was only when she threatened to go higher in their hierarchy that they agreed to take a statement.

'It's only when they realise that it's more trouble for them to do nothing than to do something that they take any notice,' she explained to her husband, as if giving him a rule to live by.

The policeman who came to take the statement listened to Mrs Finch and then began to write.

'I'll write it myself, thank you very much,' she said, who had no very high respect for the literary ability of constables.

When she finished, the policeman, who felt both intimidated by and resentful at her commanding manner, said, 'What do you want us to do about it?' as a kind of revenge. He was that new type of policeman, supposedly the master rather than the servant of the public.

'To catch the culprit, of course,' she said. 'A crime has been committed, and it's your job to find the perpetrator.'

'It could have been an accident.'

'Nonsense. My husband' — she tilted her head slightly in his direction so there could be no mistake — 'would never touch antifreeze. He doesn't even know what it is.'

'The cat could've drunk it anywhere.'

'But I've given you a suspect with a motive.'

'That's suspicion, not evidence. But if you insist, I'll have a word with your neighbours — not that it'll do any good. They'll just deny it.'

'That's the least you can do.'

The policeman went next door.

'Yes?' said Mr Rose as he opened the door.

'It's come to our notice that next door's cat has died of poison,' said the policeman.

'How's it come to your notice?' asked Mr Rose.

'I can't tell you that,' said the policeman. 'It's confidential. I'm only making enquiries.'

'What's it got to do with me?'

'The cat died of antifreeze poisoning. Perhaps it was an accident.'

'You mean probably, don't you?'

'That's as may be. I take it you didn't poison the cat?'

'Certainly not.'

'Can I take a look round?'

'Be my guest. I've nothing to hide.'

This was true: Mr Rose had already disposed of the bottle and washed the saucer thoroughly.

The policeman's search was perfunctory: most of what he did was *pro forma*, and this was no exception. He glanced round several rooms and left as if he had performed his duty.

The next time Mr Rose crossed Mrs Finch's path, when they were both emerging from their respective front doors, he alluded to the way she had called the police, as if she were an informer during the Occupation.

'I haven't the time for this,' said Mrs Finch, and drove off at speed.

Some weeks later, an official from the Public Health Department called at the Finches' house.

'You've buried a cat in your back garden?' he said.

'What of it?' said Mrs Finch, who by chance had taken the day off.

'I've had information that it might not conform to safety standards.'

'What information? What standards?'

'According to our rules, under local government powers, a cat must be buried at least four feet below the surface of the ground, at a distance of at least eight feet from a sewer, pipe or cable, and more than ten feet from any other person's property. I have reason to suspect that this may not have been the case with the burial of your cat. Can you demonstrate that it is?'

Mrs Finch hesitated between lying and telling the truth. Her hesitation was noted by the official.

'We'll have to send someone to check,' he said. 'You might need a reburial.'

When he left, Mrs Finch realised that the road ahead would be a long one, with many potholes and hairpin bends.

GETTING TO THE ROOTS

The death of Felicia Homerton just after her fifteenth birthday caused a national outpouring of grief, or at least of mourning. The piles of cellophane-wrapped flowers outside her middle-class suburban home were so high that it was almost impossible to reach the front door of the house, even for the most determined journalist. The sale of teddy bears in the three days following her death broke all records and created a shortage so that extra flights had to be laid on from China. Some of the teddy bears were found to have been stuffed with fentanyl, but as the government minister pointed out, they were only a tiny minority.

Those who lived too far away from Felicia's home to deposit their tributes there, or who could not afford the high fares of the special trains and buses laid on, established shrines to her memory in their own towns and cities, many of which rivalled in size the tribute outside her home. The following Sunday, the Archbishop of Canterbury preached a sermon on Felicia's life, drawing attention to its similarity to that of an early Christian martyr. She had died for what she believed in, he said, and could not be deflected from her purpose by the prospect of all the glories or rewards of this world.

The mourning was worldwide. Embassies and consulates opened so that people, who formed orderly lines outside, could sign books of condolence, enough soon to have filled a library. Some of the mourners did not confine themselves to signing their names but added little drawings, usually of smiling faces, and sometimes a few lines of doggerel. A publisher had the idea of buying the rights to these outpourings, published the collection quickly in several languages, and sold millions. He also published a book of photographs of Felicia from cradle to grave with gilt-edged pages.

Her death had not been unexpected, of course — death by starvation is slow and gradual — and had been followed as closely as any Brazilian follows a *telenovela*. One of the international television chains had secured the rights to place a camera in the dying girl's bedroom, but even that was not as popular as the thoughts and photos she herself posted on the social media. These were followed by six hundred million people worldwide: the advertising revenue was considerable, and Felicia's parents would never have to worry about money again. Felicia managed to keep it up — bravely, everyone said — till near the very end. It was almost a miracle, some said. Even before her death, photos of her began to appear in shops, stores and other places, usually with a little lighted candle in front of them. The managers of these establishments feared that if they did not show photographs of Felicia, they would lose custom to those establishments that did.

Candles, of course, were another commodity in short supply after her death, especially scented ones or those that floated on a little pool of essential oil. So acute did the shortage become that store owners felt obliged to ration supplies first to two, and then to one, per person. There were even reports of robberies of girls on their way to place their candles at the shrines, where there were touts selling candles of unknown provenance at inflated prices. For those who could not afford candles, there were joss-sticks, but there was soon a shortage of holders so that they were stuck into teddy bears like needles into effigies of enemies. For a few days, the centres of even the most workaday towns smelled like the interiors of eastern temples.

Felicia Homerton's funeral was watched by almost as many people as watched the final of the World Cup. It was a grandiose affair, with a glass hearse drawn by six black horses, magnificently caparisoned, the black edged by gold, and with long black plumes attached to their heads. The roads on the way to the cemetery (the route having been publicised in advance) were thickly-lined by crowds that scarcely needed to be kept in order by the red-uniformed guardsmen in black busbies who also lined the route. The crowd applauded the cortege as it went by, though some were appalled by the plumes: surely some bird or birds had been sacrificed to obtain them? A few purists were so disgusted by them, in fact, that they turned their back on the cortege, but they were a small minority. The argument that the plumes were already in existence at the time of Felicia's death did not impress them; it was a typical rationalisation, they said.

The ceremony was watched in squares and public places all around the country, relayed on huge screens erected for the purpose. The funeral was sponsored by a large fashion company famous for its jeans and its new range of what it called its non-binary fragrances. Fortunately, it was a fine day, which many took as endorsement of Felicia's whole life, though they would have been hard put to say by whom or by what. By special request of Felicia's parents, and out of respect for Felicia's views, no food or drink was on sale during the ceremony (though breast-feeding was permitted, of course). Since it was necessary, in order to obtain a good place, to arrive at least two hours before the start of the ceremony, some people had brought sandwiches with them, but when they tried to eat them suffered the disapprobation of all those around them. This was mainly expressed by hissing or commentary *sotto voce*, but in one or two places scuffling broke out and the offending sandwiches were trampled into the ground.

At last, the ceremony began and the cortege moved off from the suburban home in which Felicia had lain in state, visited only by her grandparents, uncles, aunts, schoolfriends and the first ten thousand who booked a visit on a special website. The decision to limit the numbers so severely was criticised, but as several newspaper editorials pointed out, a suburban home is hardly Westminster Abbey or St Paul's. On their visits, her uncles and aunts left money behind on her corpse, though it was hardly of use to her now: but they had no other way of expressing her importance to them, which of course was only temporary.

Immediately after her death, the local council decided unanimously to rename the road after her, as well as her school (formerly the William Shakespeare Secondary School). A film company bought the exclusive rights to her life and started to make a film with surprising celerity. The producer soon decided, however, that the house in which she lived was unsuitable and found a better elsewhere. It seemed to him more authentic.

It rained heavily for four days after the funeral, and the immense piles of flowers began to rot in the damp. Who was to clear them away? The various councils argued that it should be the charity that Felicia's parents had set up in her name even before her death, but the charity, whose trustees included a famous television character actor and a writer of children's books, said that it was up to the councils: it was their job to keep the streets tidy. The councils cleared away the flowers but sent bills for the labour involved to the charity, which refused to pay. Lawyers were instructed on both sides, but before the matter could be settled, another scandal broke. A newspaper revealed that council workers had gathered up thousands of teddy bears (and a smaller number of soft toy tigers and kangaroos) and were now selling them on their own account over the internet, and although it was unclear to whom the teddy bears rightly belonged, everyone was agreed that it was certainly not the council workers. The charity therefore launched a countersuit against the councils, who denied responsibility for what the council workers did when they were not following the councils' express instructions. The case took up much of the evening news for three successive nights.

Although Felicia's family was not Catholic, a grass-roots Catholic movement proposed Felicia for beatification as soon as possible as a first step to canonisation, expressing dissatisfaction and even outrage at the bureaucracy of the process and the rigid insistence on strict criteria for sainthood. This was not reasonable in a modern society. A committee was sent up to bring canonisation into the twenty-first century, and the Pope promised to examine its proposals with an open mind.

Two weeks after her death, there was alarm about girls of Felicia's age who were imitating her and starving themselves to death. They firmly closed their mouths against all sustenance and one of them — the first to die in her name — refused even water, on the grounds that there was soon to be a water shortage everywhere in the world, and she did not want to add to it by wasting water on herself.

To counter this dangerous trend, a conservative newspaper commissioned a series of articles suggesting that, far from having been selfless, Felicia had been a cunning little minx, but liberal newspapers retorted, wishing to preserve her legacy, that, whatever else may be said against them, cunning little minxes did not usually go to the extremity of starving themselves to death.

Felicia had become a vegetarian at the age of eight when she learned that bacon was made of the flesh of pigs killed for the purpose. It was also about that time that she saw a whole dead chicken in a butcher's shop dismembered with a cleaver. She saw its head and feet, and screamed, crying inconsolably for fifteen minutes afterwards. Further enquiries revealed to her that lamb chops were not so-called for no reason: they entailed the sacrifice of little lambs.

She was an only child and therefore, not surprisingly, much indulged. Nevertheless, there was about her, from the moment she learned to talk, a certain hardness or fixity of purpose about her which slightly disconcerted her parents. Her lips were thin, she seldom smiled, she never laughed, and her eyes had a mineral glitter to them. She was always determined to have her own way, and her little jaw would clamp shut such that nothing short of victory would prise it open. When she was seven, she sent a letter to Father Christmas: there was no possible doubt about the precocity of her mental development, and even her handwriting was unusually perfect for her age.

Dear Father Christmas [she wrote],

I don't want you to bring me anything for Christmas because I already have so many toys and some little girls have none. Please give the toys that you were going to bring me to them.

Felicia xxx

P.S. Please be nice to your reindeer and do not make them work too hard.

Her parents sent her letter to the local newspaper which printed it on its front page under the headline 'Local girl thinks only of others'. A photographer came and took a picture of Felicia feeding her hamster, Gorgeous. This photograph took up a quarter of a page of the newspaper, and naturally everyone was very proud of her. Her parents bought as many copies of the newspaper as they could find and cut a copy of the article out and pinned it to the kitchen notice-board. Her school put several copies of it on the walls, including of her classroom. The headmistress referred to the letter often, calling on other children to be as selfless as Felicia. The other children, who in truth had always been a little afraid of her for reasons that they could not explain though she had never done anything malicious, began to steer clear of her. Some of their parents began to whisper that the letter had not really been written by Felicia at all, not in the sense that she had composed it herself, and that really it was the work of her parents: though there were others who said that this was just envy that their own children were not as clever as she. But the rumours only grew stronger when the BBC took the story up, not only for its children's programme but for the evening news. They sent a well-known reporter to her home to interview her, accompanied by cameraman and sound engineer. Felicia was not at all surprised by this, nor was she abashed by it, taking it almost as her due. She spoke to the reporter, who seemed almost more in awe than she was of him, just as she spoke to her parents, with a definiteness of opinion that charmed in one so young.

'Why did you write your letter to Father Christmas?' asked the interviewer, leaning towards her solicitously.

'Some little girls have lots of toys,' she said, 'and some don't have any. That's not fair.'

'What do you think ought to be done about it?' asked the interviewer, smiling.

Felicia was very clever, and though she had not thought about it before, she was able to answer.

'I think little girls with lots of toys ought to give some to girls without any, especially in Africa.'

'And what about little boys, what should they do?'

'Little boys have lots of guns. They should throw them away.'

When she spoke, Felicia's plaits, which hung down beside

her round face, shook a little, up and down and from side to side.

The interviewer spoke to Felicia's parents afterwards. Trying not altogether successfully to disguise their pride, they said that Felicia had always thought very deeply about things and was always ready to help others.

The interview was widely praised, at least in some circles. In attacking government policy, the leader of the opposition contrasted its selfishness with Felicia's generosity. The leading liberal newspaper published a short editorial about the interview. 'It is surely a sign of our moral decay,' it said, 'that a little girl of eight should be able to enunciate a universal and simple principle that should be applied in any civilised society but which our leaders, by their daily conduct, not only ignore but violate.' The newspaper's cartoonist depicted Felicia in the robes of an angel giving a lesson to the Prime Minister, who had a tail and horns, and who wore red satin. Felicia pointed to a blackboard with the word GENEROSITY with a long pointer, saying 'Now repeat after me.'

Felicia received hundreds of letters after the interview was broadcast, and it was viewed millions of times on the internet. Someone had the idea of starting a charity, called *Felicia's Gift*, that collected unwanted toys and sent them to Africa. They poured in far quicker than they could be distributed, and the founder had to make an appeal to the public to stop sending them, otherwise they would have to be burnt. A cynical journalist discovered that not a single toy had reached Africa and that the toys were piled in complete disorder in a disused warehouse whose owner was suing the charity for rent. *Felicia's Gift* dissolved itself and faded from view. But as the journalist said to avoid the imputation of malice on his part, it was the thought that counted.

Felicia's first fame faded with the charity, but she remained very serious for her age. She became a vegetarian and tried to persuade her classmates to follow her.

'Just think it was your dog or cat that you were eating,' she said.

'That's gross!' they would exclaim, but her growing unpopularity and their tendency to avoid her when they could, did not deter her: in fact, it made her more determined than ever. And she was very good at her schoolwork.

She made her first convert in Barbara, a girl with buck teeth and too many freckles to be popular. Since she could not distinguish herself by her beauty, she decided to do so by adopting an opinion that was at first unpopular. The other girls called her stupid, but they knew that Barbara, though freckled, was not stupid. Felicia defended her stoutly.

'It's never stupid to be right,' said Felicia, her plaits trembling slightly.

At home, now that Felicia was eating with her parents rather than on her own, vegetarianism prevailed, not from any conviction on their part, but because it was simply too difficult and time consuming to prepare two types of meal every day. In addition, it was uncomfortable for parents to sit under the regard of a disapproving child whose arguments they suspected might be right. Their conscience pricked them. Their counterarguments were rationalisations, and they knew it: they were designed to allow them to indulge in their pleasures with a clear conscience. The desire for an easy life changed gradually into conviction.

One day, Felicia watched a film about a battery chicken farm. Until then she had loved eggs, but now that she had seen the conditions in which they were produced, she was revolted by them.

'But Felicia,' said her mother, 'I buy only free-range eggs. The chickens that lay them can run about.'

At first this satisfied Felicia, though before she would eat an egg, she would demand to see the eggbox from which it had come. Still suspicious, however, she found out what 'free-range' really meant. The word suggested farms of old, in which chickens roamed a farmyard, searching for food, but it meant nothing of the sort. Free-range chickens were only slightly better-off than their battery sisters.

'If chickens were male,' said Felicia, 'they wouldn't treat them like that.'

Free-range eggs, then, were forbidden the house, but Felicia's mother had an idea.

'Wouldn't it be fun to keep chickens ourselves?' she said. 'They could have the run of the garden, and we would have fresh eggs every day. Wouldn't that be lovely?'

Felicia reserved judgment but raised no objections. She insisted, however, that the three chickens came from the Abused Chickens' Rescue Centre, which specialised in reprieving chickens from death once their most prolific laying days were over.

'But Felicia, that will defeat the whole point of having them.'

Felicia maintained that if they were treated well, they would start laying again as they had before. And she proved to be right: soon they had at least three fresh eggs a day.

Felicia, however, did not feel entirely happy about gathering the warm brown eggs: she felt that it was like stealing and that they were exploiting the chickens, keeping them under false pretences. They were not being kept for their own sake but for what could be got out of them. She mentioned this to her mother, who repeated that if it were not for them, the chickens would have been dead long ago.

Then disaster struck. One evening, the door to their coop was not closed properly, and immediately seeing and seizing its chance, a fox entered and killed all the chickens. There were bloody feathers everywhere, and what was worse, the fox had not killed just for food, because it was hungry, but for the sheer joy of killing.

Naturally, Felicia was very distressed by this, though her distress was tinged with indignation. She felt that her mother should have protected the chickens more effectively. Her mother said:

'So you see, Felicia, we are not the only creatures that eat chickens. Foxes do as well.'

'That doesn't make it right,' said Felicia. 'Besides, they're foxes. They can't help what they do. We *can*.'

Felicia's mother saw the logic of her reply and was proud of her daughter's intelligence. Felicia saw her triumph and pressed it further.

'We could have allowed the chickens to fly into the trees, and then they would have been safe because foxes can't climb.'

'Chickens can't fly, Felicia.'

'All birds can fly,' said Felicia firmly. 'That's what they've got wings for. And chickens have wings.'

'But their wings are clipped so that they can't fly,' said her mother. 'They do a little operation to make sure.' Actually, she wasn't quite sure what 'they' did and hoped Felicia wouldn't ask.

'But that's cruel!' exclaimed Felicia. 'Birds are made to fly. It's as if you cut the legs off babies so they couldn't crawl.'

Despite the violence of her comparison, Felicia's mother was proud of her young daughter's ability to think. It boded well for her future.

'That's different, Felicia,' she said. 'We keep chickens because they are useful to us.'

'Well, if the only way we can keep chickens is by preventing them from flying, I don't think we should keep them.'

Felicia's plaits shook in agreement with her, and her round face hardened into a fixed expression. By now Felicia's mother knew that expression and that when Felicia wore it nothing on earth or in heaven would change the thought that lay behind it. Felicia would have a splendid career.

Eggs were forbidden from the house from now on, and Felicia's suspicions were now aroused by milk.

'Are there any wild cows?' she asked her mother one day.

'No, dear,' replied her mother.

'Why not?'

This was a question that Felicia's mother could not answer. She had never thought about it and had no idea where cows come from or how they had been domesticated. In her far-off days in biology lessons, she had learned more about peacock's tail feathers than about cows.

'Have they all been killed?' asked Felicia.

'No, dear. Or if they have, it was a very long time ago, too late to do anything about it now.'

'And why are there no boy cows?'

'There are, Felicia, they're called bulls.'

'Why don't you ever see any?'

'There aren't very many of them, and they're dangerous.'

'Why aren't there very many of them? There are as many boys as girls.'

'Farmers don't like to keep them. They're very difficult to keep. If you see one in a field, you must be careful not to enter.'

'Why?'

'Because if they see you, they might charge at you and they are very fast and big and heavy. They might trample you. *And* they have horns.'

'Don't they like us?'

'I suppose not.'

'Why not?'

'They're born like it. They like to be alone.'

'What happens to baby boy cows if they don't all grow up to be bulls?'

'Some of them become oxen. You'll have to ask a farmer, Felicia,' said her mother, growing a little exasperated.

Felicia knew that her mother was not telling the truth, which she therefore knew to be bad.

Milk was forbidden the household, and Felicia soon discovered that cheese was made of it.

A week later, Felicia asked, 'Mummy, what is leather made of?' Of course, she already knew the answer, which is why she asked.

Felicia's mother knew the answer in outline — that leather was the skin of cattle treated in some way or other — but was hazy as to detail and preferred not to think about it.

'Leather is made from the skin of cows,' she said, feeling obliged to say something.

'Before or after they're dead?' asked Felicia.

'After, of course.'

'Do they kill cows for leather?'

'No, they wait for the cows to die anyway.'

'What do they die of?'

'I don't know, Felicia.'

'And then what do they do?'

Really, it didn't bear thinking about.

'Why don't you go and play in the garden, Felicia? It's a lovely day, and I've got things to do.'

It wasn't long, of course, before leather was banned from the house. Felicia wouldn't put on her leather shoes and insisted on canvas ones.

No animal product was knowingly admitted to the house, and Felicia routinely scanned the contents of whatever was brought into it. Almost unconsciously, her mother began to do the same. She even tried to convert some of her friends and acquaintances to her point of view.

'It's terrible how they treat animals,' she would say, as if she had discovered it for herself.

Peace reigned in the household while Felicia grew into adolescence. She was short for her age, but the doctor assured her parents that she was not abnormally so.

'After all,' he said, showing them the normal curve, 'someone has to be at the lower end of it. But,' he added by way of consolation, 'Felicia's very advanced for her age in other ways.'

It was true that she was first in her class in schoolwork. She applied herself to it with a fierce intensity and was undistracted from it by the kind of other interests that led many a promising girl astray. Naturally, this did not increase her popularity, but she was not in the least put out by that, for by now she had a little party of acolytes who had followed Barbara into the fold of the righteous. They eschewed makeup because of its morally dubious provenance and the methods by which it was tested for safety.

'Poor little rabbits,' said Barbara.

'If it wasn't for make-up,' said Lydia, leader of the pre-libertine faction of the class (by far the larger), 'there wouldn't be any rabbits.'

Barbara didn't know what to reply but reported the conversation to Felicia.

'Tell her,' said Felicia, who wanted to make it sound as if Barbara had thought of it herself, 'that if rabbits are cruelly treated, it would be better if there weren't any rabbits because then there would be less suffering in the world. Rabbits are kept in little square cages so that when they are pulled out, they are square themselves. They are so unhappy it would have been better if they had never existed.'

'I'll tell her they'd be better off dead,' said Barbara.

'No, it would have been better if they had never been born,' said Felicia. 'There's a difference, you know. It's not the same thing.' She made Barbara repeat what she was going to say.

Barbara repeated the lesson to Lydia who told her to bog off and called her a silly cow.

Nevertheless, Felicia's influence in the school was growing. The balance was tipping in favour of her followers rather than of her mockers. By the time Felicia made her dramatic new discovery, about three quarters of her class, and half the school, were vegetarian. Many of the girls were determined and even militant. Whenever they saw someone eating something that was not vegan, they reacted with histrionic horror and exclaimed 'Murderer!'

When she turned thirteen, Felica came across the work of Dr Jürgen Müller, a German botanist. Dr Müller was the head of a team investigating the ability of plants to communicate with one another. They discovered, for example, that when a tomato was picked from a plant, the nearby plants drooped their leaves: not by very much, it was true — it required sophisticated instruments to detect — but the point was that they did it at all. His team went on to show that the same was true of gooseberries, green beans and peas, among others. In fact, wherever they looked for it, they found it.

They also found that a carrot pulled from the ground had some effect on its neighbours. The team carefully controlled for obvious physical effects such as disturbance of the soil. There seemed no escaping the conclusion that plants were sensitive to one another and lived in a community. Since drooping leaves were a sign of unhealthiness in a plant, it was obvious to Felicia that they suffered when one of them was separated from the rest — a kind of grief.

'Do you know that plants suffer?' Felicia asked her mother.

'Well of course they can be unhealthy,' she replied, 'if you don't water them.'

'I don't mean that,' said Felicia, with an edge of contempt in her voice. 'I mean, they can feel just like we can.'

'Don't be silly, Felicia. They don't have any nerves like ours.

And they can't hear or see anything.'

'Yes, they can,' said Felicia. 'Dr Müller's laboratory has done experiments to prove that plants speak to one another. And they have done experiments that prove that tomatoes grow better if you play them Mozart. But they suffer too if you pick their neighbours. Playing Mozart to them is a kind of lying because they are only going to be picked soon afterwards. It's cheating them, like feeding pigs.'

Felicia explained all Dr Müller's experiments to her mother. It was as if the pupil had become the teacher and *vice versa*. Her mother was not a very apt learner, though Felicia thought the lessons easy enough.

'Don't you see what that means?' Felicia would ask.

'I'm not sure I do,' her mother replied.

'It's obvious. Plants have feelings, just like us!'

'Well…' said her mother sceptically.

'What else can it mean?' asked Felicia in a challenging manner.

Her mother could not answer.

'So you see,' said Felicia triumphantly.

The first plants to be forbidden the house were cut flowers, for whose murder there could be not even utilitarian justification. Felicia said it was cruel to cut them off from their parents just as they were reaching maturity, and just because they looked pretty. There was a lot else to be said against them, of course. Mostly they were grown in highly artificial conditions, just like battery chickens. They were crowded together unnaturally and force-fed chemicals. They were like geese stuffed with food to produce *foie gras*. Greenhouses, where many plants spent their entire lives, were like prisons.

And another thing: growing flowers like that gave no opportunity for bees to do their essential work.

After the cut flowers came the pot-plants. If flowers in greenhouses were prisoners, pot-plants were in solitary confinement, as if undergoing special punishment. Theirs was a life sentence: they would never know what it was like to live in the open air.

'Most of them are not even native to this country,' said Felicia. 'They had to be brought here. They wouldn't survive in the wild.'

'Isn't that a good reason to look after them?' asked her mother.

'It's like slavery,' said Felicia firmly. 'They were uprooted from their homeland and brought here against their will.' Felicia had just done a project in school about Dahomey. 'They were brought here for our use.'

'We don't *use* them, dear,' said Felicia's mother.

'Yes, we do,' said Felicia. 'We use them for decoration. We don't think of their welfare at all.'

'We do, Felicia, I feed them regularly.'

'Chemicals,' said Felicia disdainfully.

'And I water them.'

'From the tap.'

Before Felicia's mother could ask what difference that made, water being water, Felicia explained the difference, her plaits (which she still wore) backing her up.

'Plants like to feel rain on their leaves,' she said. 'Just like us when it snows. Besides, rainwater is much purer that tap water. Tap water has all kinds of things in it.'

'What kind of things?'

'Waste medicines and hormones from plastic. They get into the water and stay there because of the way they recycle it. And then we give it to the plants! They can't do anything to avoid it. It's not fair.'

So it was easier to get rid of the plants, of which there were not many. Felicia's mother suggested that they re-pot them in the garden.

'Don't be silly,' said Felicia. 'You said yourself that they couldn't survive in the wild. It would condemn them to a slow painful death.'

'The geraniums might survive.'

'Geraniums are genetically modified. They're not natural.'

Felicia uprooted the plants and put them in the rubbish bag to be collected two days later.

Then Felicia decided that the garden was all wrong. The problem was that the plants in it were arranged as humans wanted, not as the plants wanted themselves.

'It's as though they're in a military parade,' said Felicia, 'ready to go to war. But flowers are peaceful, and so are plants. They live in harmony with one another. They don't need to be told what to do.'

'But if we don't arrange the garden, weeds will take over.'

'So what? Weeds have as much right to live as any other plants. Anyway, what you call a weed is often very pretty if you look at it right, just as pretty as artificial flowers. Really, there's no such thing as a weed.'

'Our flowers are not artificial, Felicia,' said her mother. 'We buy them in a nursery, you remember. You always come with me to choose them.'

'I was too young to realise it was wrong to grow flowers in

that way, but I do now. Flowers should be free, like humans. Plants have rights. And you can't buy humans.'

Her mother was half-angry with, and half in awe of, her only child, but as always her awe triumphed over her anger. From then on, the garden had to be left to its own devices, seeding itself spontaneously. Thistles, dock and bindweed began to take over and became the kind of garden round the houses of the very old or the mad. Felicia was very pleased.

'Now all the plants are free,' she said. 'They grow as they like.'

The neighbours complained — the street was a highly respectable one — but Felicia's mother explained that theirs was an ethical garden, which accounted for its disorder. She explained how a wild garden was more rational than a manicured one and just as beautiful when you looked at it closely or got used to it, better for the health of plants, less polluting and more insect- and therefore bird-friendly. The neighbours looked at her quizzically but did not contradict what she said openly. After all, they couldn't possibly be in favour of *more* pollution and fewer birds, let alone against wild flowers.

Then the team in Germany discovered that potatoes suffered when their fellow-tubers were pulled from the ground. By careful experiment, they demonstrated that potatoes grew more slowly after some among them were dug out of the earth.

Felicia, who was learning about the Holocaust in school, asked her mother how she would like it if she were suddenly torn away from where she had lived all her life and boiled alive with a dozen other people like her.

Her mother had to admit that she wouldn't have liked it.

Felicia wrote a letter to the main newspaper of humane opinion, pointing out our ignorant and unthinking cruelty to vegetables, especially root vegetables. It created quite a stir, and there was a small flurry of letters of support. The National Association of Potato Growers wrote an attempted rebuttal, but of course all denials go to show just how well-founded accusations are, otherwise they wouldn't be advanced. At first Felicia was elated, but before long it dawned on her that the sale of potatoes, carrots, parsnips and turnips (she hated swedes) had hardly decreased, if it had at all. Something more would have to be done if all this avoidable suffering were to be reduced.

Lettuces were next. They were still alive when you ate them. It was disgusting, appalling, when you came to think of it. Thinking of lettuces, Felicia suddenly realised that, from an ethical point of view, there was nothing that she could eat. In order for her to eat, something else had to die. Eating was killing; there was no way round it. And it was immoral to live at the expense of others.

'I'm not going to eat anything ever again,' she announced one day, her plaits jiggling angrily.

'Whyever not, Felicia?' asked her mother, thoroughly alarmed.

'Every time I eat something, some living being has to suffer and die.'

'But if you don't eat, you'll die yourself.'

'I think that'd be a good thing. I'm a parasite, all human beings are. They're a blight on the surface of the earth. The world would be much better off without them.'

'But only you will die if you don't eat, not everyone else.'

'I can set an example.'

Her mother took Felicia to the doctor. He was not very concerned.

'Young girls often have these phases,' he said, talking to Felicia's mother in private. 'They pass. It takes a long time to starve yourself to death, and in the meantime she'll change her mind. The important thing is that she should keep drinking fluids. You can't survive long without drinking, unlike eating, but very few people can resist thirst. I shouldn't worry too much if I were you.'

'You don't know Felicia,' said her mother.

'You'll see,' said the doctor confidently.

On the way home, Felicia's mother said to her, 'Promise me you'll keep drinking, Felicia.'

'It's wrong to use up water,' said Felicia categorically. 'There's a growing shortage of it.'

'But that wouldn't matter if no one used it anyway.'

'But they *do* use it and there's going to be a terrible shortage. Besides, human beings are not the only creatures that have to be considered. If the surface of the earth dries out, there won't be any life left. The world will be just sand, like the Sahara Desert.'

The doctor was right, Felicia didn't last even a day without drinking: but eating was another matter. It was as if, in the presence of food, Felicia's jaws had been clamped together.

Felicia, who was small to begin with, began rapidly to lose weight. At first, she remained energetic and even seemed more active than usual. But then she took on a gaunt or haunted air. The headmistress of Felicia's school called her mother to see her.

'There's something seriously wrong with Felicia,' she said. 'She's ill.'

'She refuses to eat. She won't let a thing past her lips.'

'Is she on hunger strike?'

'No, it's just that she says that she's not prepared to live at the expense of other life.'

'Is there anything wrong at home?' In the headmistress's experience, trouble at home was the root of all evil, at least in all pupils.

'No, my husband's a good man, he never loses his temper or anything like that.'

'I think we'd better call the psychologist.'

But the psychologist could get nowhere. All that Felicia would talk about was how to save plants and make them safer, how they had as much right to live as anybody, how farming and horticulture were depriving vegetables of their rights. This was an idea not a symptom, said the psychologist, so that there was nothing that she could do.

Felicia grew quickly weaker. Her breath soon took on that unpleasant odour of the starving, caused by the melting away of the flesh as the organism tried to maintain itself on its own resources. She spent more time in bed, her limbs having become sticks. It was as much as she could do to move about the house supported by her mother. Her father, a man contented until now to leave everything domestic to his wife, insisted that a psychiatrist be called. He was confident that the psychiatrist would take Felicia away because she was mad and force-feed her, and that in fact he should have been called long ago. But the psychiatrist was a disappointment.

Overburdened by work, it took him three weeks to come, by which time Felicia was bedridden. Coming down the stairs from her bedroom after he had spoken to her for nearly half an hour, he announced that Felicia was within her rights to starve herself to death. It was true, he said, that in the opinion of many, her ideas were exaggerated: but if you incarcerated or force-fed everyone with exaggerated ideas, you would soon have to lock up half the world. Besides, progress depended on freedom to have exaggerated ideas: all good ideas once seemed exaggerated. Would Felicia's parents have locked up Newton or Darwin? They were, after all, both cranks.

'But surely,' said Felicia's mother, 'she is too young to decide for herself to die for the sake of an idea?'

'There is no fixed age at which a young person has the capacity to decide for herself,' said the psychiatrist. 'It depends on her maturity and the coherence of her ideas — provided that her ideas are not mad, of course.'

'But her ideas *are* mad,' interjected her father.

The psychiatrist looked at him disapprovingly. 'Not according to psychiatric criteria. I myself am a vegetarian — a vegan in fact.'

In short, there was nothing he could do, and so he left.

Felicia's parents went upstairs to see their daughter. Although she was very weak, a smile of triumph played on her face.

'You see,' she said in a low voice. 'I'm not mad after all.'

But she agreed to take a sip of water as a compromise with her mother.

No one knew how the news of what the press called her fast unto death leaked out into the world. Her father removed her telephone and her computer, and anyway she was now too feeble to use them. But leak out into the world her story did, and soon her parents were inundated with offers for exclusive access to Felicia's bedroom and presumed future deathbed. At first her parents resisted the idea as repellent, but soon there was an entire encampment of journalists, cameramen and sound engineers outside the house. The neighbours complained, not to the journalists and others, but to Felicia's parents, whom they accused of destroying the peace of the street.

Her parents decided to give exclusive access to a magazine and a television company, in the hope that this would drive away the others, but in this they were deceived. A journalist disguised as a gas-inspector managed to get as far as Felicia's bedroom door. Although the door was shut, the journalist claimed to have seen and spoken to her, and he wrote a most affecting description of her condition.

Felicia gave a television interview that was seen round the world. She was so weak that even to turn her head towards the camera was a supreme effort for her. Her eyes glittered in her sunken visage, and her plaits lay motionless at forty-five degrees to her face.

'Felicia,' asked the interviewer, a young woman with splendid teeth, 'what is the purpose of your fast?'

'It's not a fast,' said Felicia.

'It's not?' said the interviewer, surprised. 'Then why are you not eating?'

'I'm not eating because it is morally wrong to eat.'

'Why is it morally wrong to eat?'

'If you eat, some living being has to die after having been

kept in terrible conditions. There are so many humans that the whole world is dying of them.'

In response to the popular admiration for her stance, Felicia's mother set up a trust in her name that would rescue cows from the need to produce anything and allow them to die in peace, only being put down in the event of painful illness. Money poured in from around the world.

The television cameras were now present in Felicia's bedroom as per the contract, twenty-four hours per day. There were hourly bulletins about her deteriorating condition, or what was called her 'progress'. Her mother became famous for encouraging her to take sips of water. Occasionally, Felicia would murmur the number of carrots or potatoes whose lives she had saved by not eating. It ran to many hundreds, if not more.

The television team remained in Felicia's room until just after the undertakers had taken her away. The company had the full rights until after her interment and rearranged the bedroom for better lighting and sound effects. Another team followed the hearse. Everyone forgot to say goodbye to Felicia's parents.

Three weeks after Felicia's death, Professor Müller was arrested in Germany. He was charged with having forged his diplomas, plagiarised his thesis, and falsified his experimental results. But there was a strong movement in his defence.

THE STING

Mrs Smith was allergic to wasps — to their stings literally, to their presence metaphorically. The latter was hardly surprising. A few years before, she had been stung by a wasp on the promenade of a seaside town. Had it not been for the fortuitous presence of a doctor who knew what to do, she would have died. Her husband's contribution to saving her life had been to chase the wasp that had stung her and to squash it angrily to death against a wrought-iron lamppost on which it had settled, either exhausted or complacent, after its labours.

The sting was what some psychologists now call a life-changing event, for the focus of Mrs Smith's life changed after it. The purpose of her life thereafter became the avoidance of wasps. Her near-death experience affected her religious beliefs. Before, she had been an assiduous congregant at a Baptist church, mainly because that was how she had been brought up; but after, she found even lukewarm belief such as hers had been absurd. How could God — or *a* God, as she now referred to him — be good if he had created wasps? What use were wasps? No one liked them. They didn't make honey, and they wouldn't be missed if they disappeared from the face of the earth altogether, quite the contrary. *And* they were dangerous as well as useless.

Not that Mrs Smith could aspire to their total elimination. Her concerns were more parochial and personal than to rid the whole world of their menace. She wanted merely to ensure that no wasp ever came near her again. Mr Smith was naturally in accord with this modest ambition, but it was more difficult than it appeared at first. In essence, it was impossible. Wasps were everywhere.

After the briefest of stays in hospital following the sting, Mrs Smith was allowed home. The doctor gave her the sternest of warnings about future encounters with wasps, told her that she must avoid them at all costs, and said that he would write to her own doctor to tell him to supply her with a needle and syringe with which to inject herself immediately in the event of being stung again. She must carry it with her everywhere, never leave home without it and never lose it. She should also be careful to replace it when its expiry date was approaching.

When she received the needle and syringe, she put a notice of its expiry date in every room, so that she could not overlook it. But this was only the least of her precautions.

She started to read about wasps: their habits, the way they reproduced, their likes and dislikes, their natural enemies (apart from her). It was not as easy to find out about them as it was to find out about bees: for less research had been done on them, perhaps because they were unattractive as well as useless or harmful. Even though bees also stung and had been known to descend on people en masse and sting them to death, they were held in general affection. Bees were furry while wasps were shiny, and people liked furry creatures.

She was horrified to discover through her researches that there were thousands of species of wasp, even if 'only' (as one article put it) two hundred and fifty of them stung. This must have meant, of course, that you were never far from a wasp, and by some kind of cosmic malignity the most common variety, the variety that spoiled picnics and landed in jam at outdoor teas, had among the worst of stings and was bad-tempered. She was pleased to learn, though, that wasps had natural enemies (apart from her), that rats and badgers even ate them, but clearly they did not do a very good job of ridding the world of wasps because they were nevertheless so numerous. There were even some perverse authors who tried to persuade the public that wasps were useful and even necessary. Mrs Smith wouldn't have minded betting that, in private and in practice, these self-proclaimed lovers of wasps avoided them just like everyone else. They claimed that they destroyed garden pests and pollinated flowers, which might well be so but was beside the point. There were plenty of other pollinators, after all, and as for destroying garden pests, the enemy of my enemy is not necessarily my friend. One did not preserve a worse pest to get rid of a lesser pest.

And then they claimed, these wasp-lovers, that wasps were admirable builders. What had that to do with it? Old-fashioned prisons built by the Victorians were often admirable from the architectural point of view, but that did not mean that you would want to let all the prisoners out or live in one yourself. Come to think of it, it was probably no coincidence that both convicted criminals and wasps were confined in cells, wasps in nests and prisoners in prisons.

The wasp-lovers even had the temerity to call some of the wasps, including the commonest and worst among them, the *social* wasps. Social, indeed! Antisocial, more like it. They, the wasp-lovers, would probably one day try to have a law passed protecting wasps from being killed, without regard for those such as she who risked death daily from an encounter with a wasp. They had no idea what it was to live in fear, and this despite the fact that many thousands of people were in the same danger as she. Some people evidently cared more for insects than for people.

Mrs Smith naturally informed herself about the precautions to be taken to lessen the chances of being stung by a wasp, and she was rather put out that her husband had not thought or bothered to do so before she did so herself. He behaved as if, having recovered from her collapse, she was cured, as if she had merely suffered a bout of pneumonia. He did not seem to realise that she lived with a burden that would last the rest of her life, even were it not brought to an end by a wasp-sting. He had always been one of those people who preferred to close his eyes to unpleasantness and believe that he had thereby made it go away.

There were many precautions to take. First, of course, it was necessary to avoid wasps at all costs; that was the most important and obvious. In fact, from now on it was Mrs Smith's main aim in life. But given the number of wasps in the world, it was not going to be easy.

'Prevention is better than cure,' Mrs Smith said to her husband, as if it were an original thought.

'Of course it is,' said Mr Smith, who never denied the undeniable.

Mrs Smith discovered (from reading) that wasps were attracted by bright colours. Never again could there be flowers in the house, but that was far from all. Their clothing henceforth must be dull. Mrs Smith gave her bright summer clothes to charity. The same went for her lipsticks and other cosmetics.

'From now on,' she said, 'I shall have to be as God made me.'

Mr Smith was a sober dresser in any case, but he had one or two jumpers that Mrs Smith adjudged attractive to wasps, and so they had to go. He also had a pale linen suit and a Panama hat of which he was fond, but Mrs Smith said that they reflected a lot of light and therefore were magnets to wasps, though he had never noticed it in all the time that he had worn them. He had never gone in for bright ties even when they were fashionable, but Mrs Smith found dots or small patches of colour in them that she said resembled flowers.

'You can hardly see them,' said Mr Smith.

'Wasps have very good vision,' said Mrs Smith. 'And because they are small, they can see small things. Besides, it's the contrast that attracts them.'

Mr Smith wondered how his wife had become expert in so short a time on the biology of wasps, but he said nothing and merely watched the disposal of his clothes.

The house, of course, had to be repainted, in colours that Mrs Smith called *dark neutral*, though Mr Smith thought them just dark. The same went for the carpets. The chintz curtains and coverings of the chairs and sofa had to be changed. The house began to resemble the interior of an undertaker's establishment, except that dark now represented life, and light death.

Evidently, wasps possessed x-ray vision as well, for Mr Smith's underwear had to be changed for something less attractive to them. When Mr Smith ventured tentatively that he thought this might not be necessary, as he was not long in his underwear without anything else, Mrs Smith said that wasps were very quick off the mark and, like foxes with chickens, would spot their opportunity straight away.

The gardens, front and back, were great hazards, of course. The safest thing was to concrete them over, ensuring that there were no cracks in which wasps could nest. Mrs Smith said that nowadays they could make concrete look like proper stone, and they could put pots with artificial flowers which looked (again these days) real. In fact, they were better than the real thing: they did not wither, were perennial and could be washed down. They did not shed petals or leaves.

'But they are highly coloured,' said Mr Smith.

'Wasps can tell the difference,' said Mrs Smith. 'They are vicious but not stupid.'

'How do they tell the difference?' asked Mr Smith.

'The scent, of course,' said his wife.

Mr Smith wondered why this did not apply to furniture coverings, but he knew that his wife was no stickler for consistency, so he said nothing. For people in the grip of an idea, logic inflames rather than soothes or reassures. He tried another tack.

'Won't they look a little odd in winter?' he asked.

'We'll bring them in and store them during the winter and replace them with evergreens. It'll save us money.'

She dismissed James, the slightly slow boy who helped them once a week in the garden.

There was much else to do. Flyscreens had to be purchased and installed for every window: without such a precaution, it would be unsafe to open them, for it was by open windows that most wasps entered houses. Mrs Smith also had the idea of installing air-lock entrances to the house, front and back, to trap any wasps that might enter by the doors.

'Won't that increase rather than decrease the risk?' asked Mr Smith, who was becoming alarmed at the cost of wasp-protection. 'You might be trapped in the air-lock with a wasp.'

'I'll always have a spray with me.'

They bought a very large supply of insecticide aerosols. Mrs Smith placed a canister on every flat surface in every room. She said it was no good having to search for an aerosol when there was a wasp about: by the time she found one, it might be too late. They also bought fly-swatters as a second line of defence, having first tried out several models for their sturdiness by sticking a peanut shell (which Mrs Smith thought was as strong as a wasp's body) to the wall and swatting it with a candidate swatter. They tried the experiment several times to ensure they made no mistake.

In each room they hung a contraption that attracted insects and fried them on electric filaments. They were to be kept on night and day. Mrs Smith also insisted on fly-papers, to be hung from the ceilings, like sticky spiral brown Christmas decorations. They had to be changed regularly, of course, for whatever it was with which they were impregnated to attract insects to them would fade in time and render them less effective. They placed a standing order with the supplier, who was surprised but obliging.

From now on, they slept under mosquito nets.

'We've never had any wasps at night,' said Mr Smith.

'There's always a first time,' said his wife, scathingly. 'For me, it would be the last time as well. Anyone would think you didn't care.'

Every morning, after her shower (which Mr Smith inspected in advance for the presence of wasps), Mrs Smith would cover herself in insect-repellent. After much research on their effectiveness in deterring wasps, she selected the best, which smelt vile.

'It is only partially effective,' said Mr Smith.

'That's better than nothing,' said his wife, 'when you're facing death.'

The smell of the repellent, a cross between creosote and fish soup, began to impregnate the house.

'We'll get used to it,' said Mrs Smith to her husband when he objected to it. 'After all, everyone used to smoke, and we didn't notice that everything smelled of cigarettes. Besides, safety comes at a price.'

They installed ceiling fans in every room, rotating day and night. Wasps didn't like air currents, said Mrs Smith, because they blew them off course and prevented them from reaching their aim, which is to say Mrs Smith. Not that she exposed herself to them: the only part of her person left open to them was her face, and this she protected by the kind of veil that women wore in the early days of open automobiles or at funerals.

Naturally, nothing that contained sugar was allowed in the house, for sugar was almost as bad as jam for attracting wasps.

Mrs Smith checked for jam whenever her husband brought home the shopping, for he had previously been rather partial to it; nor did she allow artificial sweeteners, believing that wasps couldn't tell the difference. The only fruit allowed was lemons, for grapefruit having become sweeter no longer reliably failed to attract wasps. And having always been somewhat houseproud, Mrs Smith became positively fanatical about leaving not a speck of detritus of food anywhere for them to feed upon. She insisted on smooth surfaces only that could be rubbed down with alcohol.

Notwithstanding all these sensible (and essential) precautions, Mrs Smith remained always on the alert for her insect nemeses. It would be fatal, she said, to lower her guard, and she expected her husband to follow suit. Before entering any room, she swept it with her eyes and gave it a prophylactic squirt of aerosol insecticide. Then she would sniff the air like a small animal in a world of predators. Caution was necessary, and she would enter gingerly. Only after a time, having cocked her ear for the sound of buzzing, would she accept that the room was relatively safe and enter it, unwinding a fraction.

They also installed baby alarms in every room, not to be alerted to the sound of a baby crying, of course, but to that which could signify Mrs Smith's collapse after a sting, or the mere buzzing of a wasp. Mr Smith pointed out that flies also buzzed, and thus might give rise to false alarms; but Mrs Smith said that the buzzing of flies and wasps were distinguishable, and that in any case it was better to be safe than sorry.

Wasps nevertheless entered the house, in Mrs Smith's imagination if not in more tangible form. Often the baby alarm would alert her to a buzzing which might have been tinnitus.

'William!' she would exclaim, half-stentorian and half-terrified, 'a wasp in the third bedroom!'

Their sophisticated and expensive system allowed them to locate the sound coming from any of the rooms.

Naturally, it was Mr Smith who went to investigate the possible intrusion of a wasp because it was far too dangerous for Mrs Smith to do so. He went armed with a swatter in one hand and an aerosol spray in the other. In the course of the first twenty alarms, he had swatted a single fly (and not a very large one): all the other alarms had been false — though, as his wife pointed out, it was difficult to prove a negative. Any room was millions of times larger than a wasp, and just because he hadn't found one didn't mean that there wasn't one. When Mr Smith protested mildly that it wasn't necessary to respond to all the alarms, his wife said that it was sure to be the alarm he didn't respond to that was a true alarm, possibly to more than one wasp. Mr Smith thought of only pretending to respond to the alarms, but his wife also installed closed-circuit television so that dissimulation became impossible. Sometimes the alarms sounded at night, when he was sleeping; but his wife rarely slept deeply, being always half on the alert for wasps. When she heard one, or thought that she did, she dug her husband in the ribs and sent him to investigate further. He rarely had an undisturbed night's sleep.

Unfortunately, Mrs Smith began to suffer from tinnitus, which she could not distinguish either from the sound of the alarm or wasps, and which she assumed to be one or the other. The alarms grew more frequent. When Mr Smith returned having failed to locate any wasp, she would send him out again because her tinnitus had not abated. He was now thoroughly exhausted but also horribly bored by the whole situation. To be busy but bored is a terrible fate.

'I think you should see a doctor,' said Mr Smith.

'What about?'

'You're hearing wasps everywhere when there aren't any.'

'That's a matter of opinion. Just because you can't find any doesn't mean they're not there.'

'I haven't seen a single one.'

'Wasps are clever.'

Clearly the doctor could not provide a solution to the problem if she would not consult him, but the situation could not continue. Mr Smith was so exhausted by his exertions that he could hardly think.

Perhaps he could just leave his wife, but that would be cruel and unfair, as well as difficult and expensive. They had been married a long time, and before all this wasp business he had no complaints of his wife and had even loved her. They were not badly off, but separation at their time of life would be a recipe for mutual impoverishment. Their house, if sold, would raise enough for a tiny flat for each of them: but even merely to think of dividing their possessions, finding somewhere to live, and moving, exhausted Mr Smith.

'William, a wasp!'

Mrs Smith's familiar exclamation interrupted his musings.

'Where?' he asked.

'Second bedroom.'

He trudged off like a man under sentence.

'William!'

'What?'

'You've forgotten to take the swatter. You're growing careless. We can't afford to be careless.'

He returned and took the swatter.

'I can't go on like this,' he thought, as he went off on yet another wild wasp-chase, as he called it (in the privacy of his own mind, of course).

Gradually, slowly, he formed an idea. One day, he said to his wife that he was going out for a little fresh air, a walk in the park. It was a long time since he had been anywhere except the local shops.

'It's a nice day,' said Mr Smith, as if in explanation of his unusual decision.

'Don't be long,' said his wife, fighting an inclination to forbid him. 'If I should be stung while you're away...' One thought led to another. 'Perhaps from now on, we should have our groceries delivered.'

Mr Smith agreed. That would give him a standing excuse to go to the park. His wife could hardly deny him that smallest of privileges.

With great care not to be observed by her, he took two small jars with him to the park. In one, he put some jam — raspberry jam — which he had surreptitiously bought and hidden in the garage. The other he left empty.

He went to the most flourishing of the flowerbeds in the park and placed the pot containing the jam on the ground nearby and waited. Wasps always arrived at picnic: surely, they would come for jam? He took a book which he had conspicuously shown his wife that he was taking with him and began to read. He was soon rewarded. A wasp arrived, investigated the jar a little and then entered, soon getting stuck in the jam as if it were glue. Mr Smith realised that he would have to be quick if he were to trap a wasp in the other jar before it stuck in the jam. And on this occasion, only one other wasp arrived before he felt that he had to return home to avoid his wife's disapproval or suspicion, and he had failed to capture it. But he was not downhearted: nothing worked the first time round. On the way home, he scooped out the wasp in the jam with a teaspoon he had brought with him and discarded it in a litter bin.

'It was very nice in the park,' he said when he returned home. 'I must say, they keep it very well.'

He congratulated himself on having replaced the jam and the other jar in the garage without his wife having noticed.

From now on, he went to the park every day that it was fine. He never lingered long so that his wife could not object or complain. And on the fourth occasion he succeeded in trapping a wasp. But on the way home, he began to hear a buzzing emanating from the jar. Clearly this would be a problem.

But *nil desperandum*, especially in circumstances such as Mr Smith's. A little research established that there was an insect anaesthetic that entomologists used to put insects to sleep for thirty minutes or so without killing them. He purchased some, claiming that he was an amateur entomologist. You had to put a stick with a bit of cloth on the end that was impregnated with the anaesthetic and then close the lid. You had to be deft, otherwise the wasp would escape. It took some practice, but Mr Smith became quite adept at it. He took jars with sleeping wasps back to the house, first to the garage to check how long before they woke up and then remained silent. Like humans, it took them a little while to recover fully from their anaesthetic, which was all to the good.

Now he was ready for a full trial of his scheme. One day he released a sleeping wasp into the second bedroom. He waited tensely for it to wake up and become active. For once he was as alert to the sound of buzzing as his wife. Come on, he thought, start buzzing! Surely its simple nervous system would soon start to work again.

'William!' exclaimed his wife. 'There's a buzzing in the second bedroom. I'm sure it's a wasp!'

'You always think it's really a wasp this time,' said Mr Smith, trying to show his normal sangfroid.

'I'm certain of it. Don't forget the swatter.'

He needed no reminding: he knew this time that the hunt was real. In fact, he was slightly scared himself. He didn't have the same terror of wasps as his wife, but he couldn't say that he actually liked them. In fact, he had had to screw up his courage to entrap them.

He went upstairs, aerosol and swatter at the ready. He entered the room gingerly because he knew that it contained a wasp. He looked round nervously. At first, he saw and heard nothing. It was absurd to think that a wasp could think of and plan vengeance, but that is nevertheless what he did think, though he tried to put it out of his mind. Or perhaps the wasp was merely groggy after its anaesthetic. Then he saw it, settled on a curtain. He didn't want to spray it there with the aerosol because it might leave a stain on the fabric and obviously a curtain was not a good place to swat a wasp because it would give way under the blow. He decided to wait for the wasp to move under its own volition: to stir it might anger it, and even if he would not die from a sting, he had been stung as a child and had found it very unpleasant.

'William!' came a cry from below. 'What are you doing?'

'There's a wasp here,' he shouted back. 'I'm trying to kill it.'

'Be quick! Don't let it escape!'

'I'm trying. It's not easy.'

The wasp began to move. It seemed to be preparing itself for take-off. Then it did take off. Mr Smith followed its trajectory anxiously.

It flew around for a bit — searching for what, wondered Mr Smith? — and then the wretched creature settled on the ceiling. It was as if it were intelligent, knowing that it was being chased and determined to make a fool of Mr Smith.

It took off again and settled on a wall next to a black and white photograph of his wife's parents. It would be difficult to swat it there without risking damage to the picture, but Mr Smith felt obliged to try all the same. He swung the swatter back and brought it down with a crash, more or less where the wasp had been. The wasp, as if apprised of his intention in advance, had flown off, but Mr Smith caught one side of the picture frame and dislodged the picture. It fell and its glass shattered when it hit the ground.

'What's going on, William?' Mrs Smith shouted from below. 'What's happening?'

She thought it might even be her husband collapsing, having been stung by the wasp.

'Nothing,' he shouted back. 'I'm just trying to get the wasp…'

His gaze was fixed on the wasp. He did not want to let it out of his sight, for it might not be easy to find it again. But this time the wasp, perhaps over-confident, settled on a blank expanse of wall, and Mr Smith had a perfect opportunity. The swatter came down on the wasp, and there was a satisfying crunching sound as its abdomen was crushed against the wall, albeit leaving a smear. The dead wasp fell to the ground.

'Got it!' cried Mr Smith to his wife. 'Do you want to see it?'

'Certainly not!' replied Mrs Smith. 'Wasps can sting even after death. Get rid of it!'

Mr Smith flushed it down the lavatory, having suspended it by a wing like an executioner used to hold a head after a beheading (Mr Smith had heard that wasps could still sting after they were dead even before his wife told him). Then he wiped the wall on which the wasp had met its end, swept up the glass of the picture frame, and turned to his wife in triumph.

'That's one less wasp in the world,' he said.

'There are plenty more,' said Mrs Smith, unimpressed. 'Just because you've killed one doesn't mean that we don't still have to be careful.'

Mr Smith was certainly not complacent; on the contrary, he was diligent and watchful. It was necessary to get his wife used to the idea that wasps really could enter the house so that, if by chance she recovered from a sting, it would seem natural to her that there should have been a wasp to sting her in the first place. Mr Smith became an expert wasp-hunter.

From then on, wasps appeared regularly in the house in various rooms but never in the room in which Mrs Smith happened to be. Finally, Mr Smith was ready for the *coup de grâce*: for really it was pitiful to see his wife in a permanent state of terror. She could hardly sleep or eat for anxiety, and no distraction from her fear was possible for more than a quarter of an hour. It was no life at all for her.

On the day in question, Mr Smith succeeded by stealth in introducing two wasps neatly under a cushion on her chair. He placed them in such a way that they would not be squashed when she sat on the cushion. By now, he could time perfectly a wasp's recovery from its anaesthetic.

It worked perfectly. Only a minute or two after she had returned from making a cup of tea, a wasp emerged and stung her on the thigh.

'William!' she screamed. 'I've been stung! Quick, get a syringe.'

Mr Smith stood rooted to the floor. He looked at his wife as if staring at a rock.

'William! The syringe!'

Her voice was weaker now. But still Mr Smith did not move.

'William, I can't breathe!'

Mrs Smith's lips and tongue swelled, and her throat closed. She turned from pink to white and blue. She slumped in the chair. Soon she was dead.

Before he called the ambulance, Mr Smith injected his dead wife with a syringe. He explained to the ambulance men as they made their *pro forma* efforts at resuscitation that his wife had been allergic to wasp stings but that the injection had not worked. He killed the offending wasp as evidence to show the ambulance men.

'The swine!' he muttered in his distress as he did so.

The inquest took place two and a half years later because of a backlog of cases, by which time everyone had forgotten everything, except Mr Smith, of course. The coroner's verdict was death by misadventure.

REDRESSING THE BALANCE

Fortunately, the two sisters agreed about the division of their mother's belongings after she died, unlike Sylvia's best friend, who had fallen out permanently with her brother over a statue of the Buddha that their father had brought back from the East many years before and that each of them claimed that their mother had promised them. In the end, just before the case went to court, they accepted a legally binding compromise: rotating guardianship, so that the statue spent four months in their homes before being handed over to the other for four months. So badly soured had the relations between them become that, at the changeover, they had to leave the statue in a 'neutral' place to avoid meeting each other in person. Of course, the legal costs before they came to this arrangement had eaten up much of their inheritance; and Sylvia was determined to avoid such an imbroglio, so she acceded to most of her sister's wishes, which were in any case reasonable.

It is a melancholy task to divide someone's possessions after her death. One must not appear too eager, both for appearance's sake and to retain one's self-respect. This is especially true if there is something one really covets. It is important to make it look as if the demise of the departed is uppermost in one's mind: at least, if one is a decent person. Sylvia and her sister were decent people.

Whenever Sylvia's sister said that she 'wouldn't mind' having this or that, she always added, 'That is, if you're quite sure you don't want it.'

'No, no,' Sylvia would say, 'take it if you like it.'

Neither of them wanted to appear eager or as if they had thought about the division before their mother's death, though this was unlikely because their mother had been very ill for a long time and because, human nature being what it is, both of them had in fact thought about it. Therefore, they danced a kind of *pas de deux* around the things in the now eerily uninhabited house, sharing this and that between them.

Of the two, Sylvia's sister had the more definite desires. Sylvia was more interested in the sentimental than the aesthetic or monetary value of things. Monetary value didn't come into it for her (these days in any case everyone wanted new rather than old, and dealers would probably have charged to take the things away). Sylvia, who had been more attached to their mother than her sister, could not bear to think of any of her mother's belongings dispersed in an impersonal way, being indissolubly linked in her mind with her mother's whole life. To abandon her things to third parties was almost to abandon her, or at any rate to imply that she had lived in vain. It was unthinkable, especially so soon after her death; therefore, everything would have to be preserved.

An observer, no doubt, would have noticed a variation in the aesthetic quality of what her mother left behind. Some things were elegant, others were worse than ordinary. But for Sylvia, it was association with the past that lent beauty, and she did not mind that her sister, accommodating as ever, chose all the best things for herself.

Sylvia's husband, James, pointed out that they had no need of furniture, that they had everything that they could possibly need or want. After all, they had been married a long time, and it would have been strange if they had waited for an inheritance to furnish their house. Indeed, the very idea seemed humiliating to him. Besides, he added, her mother's furniture would clutter the house. He refrained from saying the word 'abominably'.

'But we could get rid of some of what we have,' said Sylvia, 'to make room for it.'

'But…' said James, who did not want to reveal to his wife just how much he did not want her mother's furniture. 'That would mean a lot of disruption, two removals in fact.'

This was true; Sylvia had hardly thought of it. Moreover, she loved her husband, as he did her. They were accustomed to compromise.

'There is so much here,' said James, looking round his mother-in-law's house. He did not add that most of it was very dark and heavy.

'Perhaps if I could take just one or two pieces,' said Sylvia. 'For their sentimental value.'

James jumped at the idea.

'The perfect solution,' he said.

'I know which ones I want.'

'Which?' asked James. He had an anxious premonition.

One of the two was a large dresser situated in the former

dining room. It was taller than a man, its wood almost black with age. It had been cobbled together by some rustic carpenter, perhaps a century and a half before, whose main idea had been solidity rather than elegance. It did indeed look indestructible — unfortunately. Like the insects, it would probably have survived a nuclear war.

James was a self-controlled man, but on this occasion his face betrayed him. A look of horror passed over it, which he made a conscious effort to overcome: the look, not the horror.

'You don't like it?' said Sylvia.

This was an understatement that produced turmoil in James's breast. He did not just dislike it, he loathed and detested it. He had done so ever since he had first set eyes on it when Sylvia presented him to his mother-in-law to be. He did not understand how anyone could have bought it even under the direst necessity (and could a dresser ever have answered a dire necessity?). A purchase always involved choice, and to have chosen nothing would have been far, far better than this.

How could anyone not notice how hideous it was? The carving on the lower doors, which of course did not close properly without extraneous assistance, not because of age or use but because they had not been made properly, was crude and resembled hacking at wood more than it resembled carving. The racks for crockery were similarly ill-made, but worst of all was the cantilevered upper cupboard to which a net-curtain arrangement had been tacked.

Like many ugly things, it was large and dominating, even domineering. Its ugliness appeared to increase its size. It was impossible to overlook or forget its presence: the looming and protruding cupboard at its top gave it almost an air of menace, as if it would suddenly spring on whoever was in the room and take him captive. If a piece of furniture could ever be evil, thought James to himself, this was it.

'I know you don't like it,' said Sylvia, 'but it means a lot to me. I remember it from my childhood.'

Sylvia's childhood had been an extremely happy one.

'It was there during all our meals and my birthday parties.'

'Isn't there anything else you'd prefer to take?' asked James, without much hope. 'It *is* very large.'

'It's the most important for me. It has the strongest memories associated with it.'

James was not an unreasonable man. He knew that human happiness did not really depend on the presence or absence of possessions.

'You'll get used to it,' said Sylvia.

'All right,' said James, forcing himself to smile. 'I know I will.'

The analogy that he had in his mind was that of a bad smell. After a time, even the worst bad smell ceased to obtrude itself on your consciousness. It was not so much that you got used to it as that you ceased altogether to notice it.

They arranged for a removal firm to bring the dresser to them; it was far too heavy for them to move themselves. Whoever made it obviously did so without thinking that it would ever be removed from where it was first erected. People in those days did not move about like they do now.

'Where do you want it?' asked the chief removal man.

'The dining room, if you don't mind,' said Sylvia. It was not quite certain where the removal man's responsibilities ended, but he was obliging.

The dresser was like an inert but nevertheless refractory giant animal that passively resisted being moved from wherever it was. It had to be wrestled rather than merely pulled, pushed, slid or carried. The removal men (there were two of them) broke out in a sweat; they coaxed it and swore at it when it did not respond. They were angry with it, and when finally it was in place, they refused a cup of tea. If they had known, they wouldn't have taken the job; they wanted to forget it as soon as possible.

'See,' said Sylvia once they had gone, 'it doesn't look too bad.'

The dark dresser now dominated their dining room, as it had dominated that of Sylvia's mother. Although the room was well-lit, and the dresser, considered mathematically, occupied only a small proportion of the cubic space, it seemed to have the effect of extinguishing light and to bring a positive quality of darkness with it. Even in midsummer, it drew the evenings on.

'You might even get to grow fond of it,' said Sylvia lightly.

'I might,' said James.

The day the dresser came to stay, Sylvia cooked a special meal to celebrate and to console James, who had always liked his food and was rarely distracted from enjoyment of it. But somehow the meal was a failure; James remained preoccupied, and his brow furrowed.

'What's the matter?' asked Sylvia, not really wanting to know.

'Nothing,' said James. 'Why do you ask?'

They both knew, but Sylvia thought that he would soon fail

even to notice the dresser. Her husband, after all, was a sensible man, not by nature given to excesses of emotion. She remembered that, long ago, when she had suggested moving, he had quoted Horace: they change their skies, not their souls, who run across the sea. He had always said that if they were happy (really and truly happy), they would be happy wherever they lived. If that was true of a house or a town, surely a mere piece of furniture could not destroy their lives.

James told himself something similar, though he suspected it was not true. He was not really an aesthete, at least not in the way of some people he knew who made living in beautiful surroundings the principal object of their lives and whose equanimity was destroyed by the slightest deviation not merely from good but from the best taste. On the other hand, he was not completely indifferent to beauty or its opposite. He had in his time even bought one or two pieces that struck him as exceptional, though he had not done so for a long time. He reflected that it was one of the ironies of life that you could afford to buy beautiful things only when there was comparatively little time left to enjoy them, or once it ceased to matter so very much. He had long since thought that he and his wife should acquire no more possessions, certainly not this dresser.

James was a man who thought that all emotion could and should be controllable. In fact, he prided himself precisely on his control. He deplored, and sometimes pitied, beings of extravagant emotion or emotional expression. After all, a man was but a single member of an insignificant species on the surface of an insignificant planet circling an insignificant star in an insignificant galaxy, and so on *ad infinitum*. Was there anything, therefore, worth working yourself up about when your life was but a drop in the bucket — no, the ocean — of time? It was ludicrous, then, to feel strongly about a mere piece of furniture.

After all, most of the time he could avoid it. The dining room was used only for meals, and not even for all meals, only for dinner or Sunday lunch if they invited someone. Dinner lasted at most an hour, usually less, so that even if he spent the rest of his time at home, at least twenty-three of the twenty-four hours in a day would not be spent in its presence. He took his phone with its calculator to work out what percentage that was: 95.3 recurring; in the old days, he would have been able to work it out in his head. Surely nothing could be intolerable for just over four per cent of the day?

This was all very well in theory, but James found that he could not order his feelings like a sergeant-major with his recruits. On the contrary, they — or at least one of them — began to master him rather than the other, correct, way about. He worried that one day the expression of his emotions might escape his control altogether, and he had long devoted his life to the avoidance of conflict.

A strange kind of rage, new to him, now inhabited him. At first, he was aware of it only in the actual presence of the dresser, that is to say in the dining room. He would grit his teeth and say nothing, but sometimes he could feel his fists clenching and his entrails knotting: they did so without any direction from his conscious mind, and he discovered them as he might have discovered a growth under the skin. Never a loquacious man, he was aware that, in the presence of the dresser, his utterances had become curt, often without a vowel. Was Sylvia aware of this? She didn't appear to be, or at any rate said nothing.

'You see,' she said cheerfully a week after the dresser's arrival, 'it isn't so bad. You're used to it already. One day you'll even come to like it and miss it if it weren't there.'

James kept silent, apart from a faint grunt. He did not trust himself to lie convincingly.

If the dresser could not be avoided altogether, the time spent in its presence could at least be reduced to a minimum. Until its arrival, it had been James' habit to wait in the dining room for Sylvia to bring the food from the kitchen to the table. This was old-fashioned, perhaps, but it suited them both. Sylvia said that he got in the way in the kitchen and his efforts at assistance merely added to, or even doubled, her work. She might on occasion have suspected that his uselessness was affected, but she generally dismissed this thought from her mind. But a couple of weeks after D-Day (as he secretly designated the day on which the dresser had invaded the house), he suggested to her that instead of waiting in the dining room as usual, he should help her in the kitchen. That way, at least, he would not be alone with the dresser.

'Why?' asked Sylvia.

'Well,' said James, 'I'm retired and do nothing all day. It's not right that you should continue as if I were still working.'

Sylvia had always been a housewife, though she had trained as a teacher. She had sometimes done voluntary work, but that was all. She was not pleased with James' suggestion with its possible implication that she was not coping because of her age.

'Thank you, dear,' she said. 'It's very kind of you, but I can manage.'

So his solitary communion with the dresser would have to continue for now. He started to take an aperitif, which he had never done before. Sylvia noticed.

'Why not?' he said to himself as helped himself to a second. 'After all, I don't have to get up in the morning any more or be clear-headed for anything.'

But even a couple of stiff gins could not disguise the lowering presence of the dresser.

He next suggested that they should not eat in the dining room. It was a lot of work for her, he said to his wife, to bring the food to the table and then clear away, and they had reached the age at which they should simplify life as much as possible. His words sounded absurd to him even as he uttered them. He was not therefore surprised when Sylvia made light of them.

'It's no trouble at all,' she said. And then she gave him a lecture on the art of growing old.

'We mustn't let standards slip, James, just because we are pensioners. You've seen that happen to the Phillipses.'

'No.'

'Yes, you have. You remarked only last week how unkempt old Phillips was looking. You said he must have worn his shirts several days running, and he was beginning to smell. He'd got bits of dried food on his jumper. Marjorie Phillips says she's cutting down on all unnecessary work, but that means necessary work too. Marjorie was never really very keen on it in the first place, if the truth be told, and I think she drinks. You wouldn't want us to live like them, would you?'

James had to admit that he would not.

'Well then, we have to be aware of slippery slopes and avoid them.'

There was no escaping, then, the baleful regard of the dresser: for regard it seemed increasingly to James to be, as if it were some malign, slow predatory creature watching for its opportunity to pounce and consume him.

Though James had always been a slow and deliberate eater, he now began to bolt his food in order to get dinner over with as soon as possible. Sylvia noticed.

'You'll give yourself indigestion if you eat like that,' she said.

'I have something I want to finish doing,' he said as an excuse to leave the room.

But he had to wait for Sylvia, who continued to eat at her normal pace. He fidgeted, which was not normal for him.

'What do you have to finish?' asked Sylvia.

'I have to write to my brother.'

He had never been close to his brother, and contacts between them had been sporadic at most.

'Surely it can wait?' said Sylvia.

'I want to do it while I still think of it,' said James, realising the weakness of his reply.

'If it's that important, surely you'll remember it later?'

In truth, James had nothing urgent to do — except escape the dresser.

But soon it was not simply a matter of leaving the dining room. The presence of the dresser seemed to expand through the house. At first, James made sure to keep the door to the dining room closed, but then he grew reluctant even to pass its door. Of course, it could not be avoided altogether: theirs was not so large a house that any part of it could be completely shut off from the rest. When he went past the dining room's door, James turned himself sideways and slid quickly past, as if to make himself as difficult and as moving a target as possible.

James tried not to let Sylvia see him behave in this way: whenever he thought that she might be observing him he would, with a supreme effort, try to pass the dining room door (which he kept always closed) as normally as he could. But it was difficult to be always vigilant, and one day she saw him sidling in this strange fashion past the door.

'What on earth are you doing, James?' she asked.

'What do you mean?' replied James, as if unaware of anything abnormal in his conduct.

'You're creeping about as if terrified of something.'

'Don't be silly. What is there to be afraid of?'

'I don't know. That's what I'm asking.'

It was all right for her to be so casual, thought James; the dresser wasn't threatening her or making her life miserable, but one day it would topple over and crush *him*. The dresser looked at him with malignity: their detestation was mutual. It was very heavy and had taken beefy removal men to shift it, only just managing to avoid an accident. And the dresser didn't even have anything particular against *them*.

'It's the dresser, isn't it?' said Sylvia. 'You're trying to avoid it.'

James tried to laugh, but it came out like dried leaves in the wind and sounded false.

'Whatever gave you that idea?'

'I've seen you do it more than once,' said Sylvia.

'You've been spying on me,' said James, trying to change

the subject and the burden of accusation.

'Nonsense,' said Sylvia firmly. 'We live in the same house, not a palace. How could I avoid noticing you?'

'I feel like I'm being watched.'

There was now an atmosphere between them that James attributed to the evil influence of the dresser. He took to his study: goodness knows what he does there, thought Sylvia. He had never been a man of wide interests, and his retirement was always certain to be a problem. If only her mother had died earlier while he was still in work, he wouldn't have made such a fuss about the dresser. He probably wouldn't even have noticed it.

One day she found a small, almost empty bottle of vodka in a drawer of his desk. James had never been a drinker before. She said nothing, for to have revealed her discovery would only have reinforced his belief that she was spying on him. Fortunately, when he drank, he was only morose, not aggressive or violent: hardly noticeable, in fact.

They now led separate lives, neither of them happy. They had always lived contentedly rather than ecstatically, but now James had a serious complaint against her. It was she, after all, who had introduced the dresser into the house though he had made his dislike of it abundantly plain at the time. She had insisted on it, in fact, as if she were in league with it; there was no other explanation of her obstinacy and insistence. The alleged sentimental value was only a pretext: there was a limit to the amount of ugliness that sentiment could overcome, and the dresser clearly exceeded it. Anyone could see that. He didn't know what Sylvia had against him — he had always been good, if admittedly a little dull; he knew it and couldn't deny it — but there must have been something. This was certainly not how he had imagined or planned his retirement.

It must have been the dresser that accounted for it. Only superficially was it an inanimate object: its influence commenced with its arrival, if not before. When he looked back, he could see that it had acted on his late mother-in-law in a similar way. She had never been happy and had always suffered from various vague complaints that no doctor had ever been able to diagnose, and *that*, he now remembered guiltily, had always irritated him. She had always been inclined as well to vague suspicions. He now realised that it wasn't altogether her fault, but it was too late to make amends. However, he could at least prevent further malignity emanating from the dresser. It had nearly destroyed his marriage, but if it thought it could get away with it, it had another thought coming. Sylvia would no doubt be angry at first, but she would get over it, come to her senses and see that he was right. Part of the dresser's technique was to cloud the judgment of the household in which it insinuated itself.

It needed to be stopped once and for all. Removal to somewhere else by sale or donation would solve his and Sylvia's problems, but only by transferring them to someone else. That would be a vile thing to do, like selling a car known to be dangerously defective. Total destruction was the only solution.

Sylvia had now taken to drawing classes every Tuesday morning. She had no great talent, and not even any great interest, in drawing, and it was too late to develop even minimal skill in it, but it was a pleasing distraction from the increasingly tense atmosphere in the house. A Tuesday morning, then, would be just the time for James to act.

He bought a large electric saw and an axe. He smuggled them into his study on a Tuesday morning. He slid them under the chaise longue and made sure that they could not be seen from the door. Sylvia no longer entered his study regularly, leaving it to gather dust. It would be very bad luck if she noticed the saw and the axe before he had time to use them.

As soon as Sylvia had left for her drawing class the following Tuesday morning, James sprang into action. The saw was for dismembering the dresser, the axe for splintering it beyond the possibility of repair. Though the dresser was not inanimate, strictly speaking, it was at least almost immobile, and would not be able to evade James' actions. Destruction was a duty, vengeance a pleasure.

James plugged the saw in and set to work. He started on a shelf, having first removed the faience plates on it, against which he bore no animus. Their association with the dresser was not their fault. As he sawed, the sawdust pleased him. How the saw must have pained the wood! But after a little while, he grew tired of the saw: he wanted a more violent chastisement of the evil thing. He took up the axe and swung it at the dresser. It was so large that he didn't really need to take aim; he swung almost at random. At first, he seemed to do it little damage, so he took more violent swings at it.

The dresser was not fixed to the wall, and it was top-heavy. James did not notice that it shuddered as he struck it. He was in no state to notice anything, so great was his exhilaration.

'Take that!' he shouted as he struck with his maximum of force (until then, he had held back very slightly).

The dresser shuddered and then toppled. James could not take evading action, and he was crushed underneath its weight. The worst and heaviest part fell on his head.

When Sylvia returned from her drawing class, she found James trapped under the dresser. The ambulance men had difficulty in extricating him. He was not dead but breathing stertorously.

A few days later in the hospital, the doctor asked Sylvia whether the machines that were keeping James nominally alive should be turned off, as to continue was futile. Sylvia agreed.

James had not done such damage to the dresser that it was irreparable. Sylvia found a joiner and cabinetmaker to restore it. He charged more than the dresser was worth, but after all, it was of sentimental value.

PUNCTUATION MARK

The two elderly men had been friends since their college days, but their friendship had been tinged by rivalry from the first, such that they always talked for victory and were never quite frank with one another. Irony concealed their real thoughts and feelings, which were perhaps unknown even to themselves, except that each secretly thought himself the superior of the other.

They had each followed a literary career, though of a different kind. One, Herbert, had been a professor, a noted scholar of Dryden and Pope, and had written the standard book on the influence of the first on the second. The other, Francis, had been the literary editor of one of the best weeklies, whose heyday was long past. Herbert thought Francis a mere journalist who had sullied or even prostituted his abilities in a search, if not for fame, at least for power and influence: for in the days of his pomp, Francis had been courted by publishers and even by authors for what in those days was still called 'the favour of a review'. Francis had attended literary parties but in doses calculated to render his attendance at them an event in itself and that assured him a fawning reception. In Herbert's opinion, Francis had insufficiently understood that his importance, like that of a British monarch, had resided in his function rather than in his person; a literary editor is the object of flattery, whatever his personal qualities or lack of them. Not surprisingly, then, according to Herbert, his decline had set in when the review of which he was the literary editor began its long death throes.

By contrast, Herbert considered himself the keeper of the flame, that of pure disinterested scholarship whose findings, albeit of interest to an infinitesimal (though discriminating) minority, were durable. His book was a monument that could never be superseded. The infrequency with which it was read, by comparison with the number of times a weekly was read, was almost a proof of its value. Francis, however, did not share Herbert's estimate of the worth of his *magnum opus*. What Herbert took as proof of purity, Francis took as evidence of pedantry. After all, literature was not, or ought not to be, a secret garden into which only the initiated and the learned might enter. It was open to all who paid the entry fee of intelligence and sensitivity, who were numerous if not predominant in the population. Francis was not such a democrat that he thought that all men were equal, at least in ability, but he was no intellectual or social snob: not for him all the apparatus of learning that intimidated more than it enlightened. He believed, or flattered himself, that in his literary pages he had struck the right balance between accessibility and high quality.

Herbert, on the other hand, did not take so sanguine a view of Francis's work. He was against compromise in the matter of scholarship, and any assertion that either was not, or could not have been, footnoted was to him anathema, an intellectual abomination, a retreat from the highest achievable standards. A published avoidable error, no matter how minor, was to him the beginning of the slippery slope towards anarchy, the kind of anarchy in which ignorant persons claimed that their opinion on a subject was the equal of that of a man who had spent a lifetime studying it. Any article that had not been examined and referenced like a doctoral thesis was not worthy of serious consideration.

Naturally, neither man told the other what he secretly thought of the other's work.

Both men were widowers in their seventies. Their literary careers had always meant more to them than had their personal lives, and their relations with their children (two each), while amicable enough, were somewhat distant. As is so often the way, the children's interests were completely different from those of their fathers, even opposed to them, as if each child had been determined to escape from his father's shadow. This was absurd, of course, based upon a misunderstanding on their part: for literature was of universal import.

For many years, almost as a ritual, they had met for lunch once a month in an old-fashioned Hungarian restaurant, still furnished as it had always been with red-plush and gilt banquettes and furnishings that absorbed noise. This permitted, even encouraged, discreet conversation. It was a haven of stability in a world that was rapidly changing, always for the worse. The public now wanted noise rather than discretion, in order to fill, so Herbert said, the vacuum that was its mind.

They always had a table to themselves, not quite but nearly a cubicle. Ferenc, the head waiter, had grown into late middle-age with them. His slicked-back black hair was now straked with iron grey; having been very tall, he now had the stoop that tall and thin men often develop with age, particularly if their occupation requires a certain obsequiousness. He offered the two men advice on what was best today as if he were imparting confidential information, specially to them and to no one else.

'The quenelles of pike are very good today,' he would say.

It would, of course, have been churlish if at least one of them had not accepted the proffered confidential advice.

'I always find the taste of freshwater fish a little muddy,' said Herbert, as he fastidiously took another fork of his quenelle.

'Then why did you order it?' asked Francis.

'*Nostalgie de la boue*, I suppose.'

'The distasteful always has its attractions,' said Francis, taking a spoon of his goulash soup with dumplings.

'Especially in our times,' said Herbert.

'Oh, I don't know about that,' said Francis, who of course agreed with Herbert on this point. 'Think of Sade or Baudelaire or Rabelais.'

'They're French,' said Herbert, as if that invalidated the point.

'What about Swift?' asked Francis. 'Surely, he was their equal?'

'I do not think you can call Swift attracted by the distasteful. It was part of reality, and he was disgusted by it.'

'Is that not the point? Attraction and repulsion are two sides of the same coin.'

'Anyway, Swift was Irish.'

'Anglo-Irish.'

'Is nationality important in literature?'

'You, not I, brought it up.'

Ferenc cleared away the plates, and with them the discussion. A new young waiter, an East European of some description, brought the main course.

'The veal?' he asked.

'For me,' said Herbert.

'The pork?' he asked after he had put the plate before him.

'Surely the deduction is not difficult,' said Herbert, as if the waiter had been an obtuse student.

'He is new here,' said Francis.

'Logic surely does not depend on experience,' said Herbert.

The two men began to eat, sipping some heavy red wine between mouthfuls.

'The veal is very good,' said Herbert, pronouncing an unarguable judgment.

'Personally,' said Francis, 'I have given up veal, or am thinking of doing so.'

'How so?' asked Herbert, between two of his precise mastications. He would not have ventured a longer sentence with his mouth full.

'The manner in which it is produced" said Francis.

'Doctor Johnson loved veal.'

'With plums.'

'The plums are immaterial.'

'In Doctor Johnson's day, meat was produced in a different way. It was less unnatural.'

'Surely the more fundamental point is that the calf was

taken from its mother, which must have distressed her as greatly as it does today.'

'The calf would have been killed immediately after separation, not kept in abominable conditions so as to make its flesh pale.'

'You mean, a short but happy life?'

'At any rate, better than today's.'

'Do you really know that? The study of eighteenth-century animal husbandry and meat production has hardly been yours.'

'They did not have the means to produce meat by modern methods.'

'I doubt that the way in which they slaughtered cattle was superior to ours. To the contrary.'

'Doctor Johnson was a very humane man with a delicate conscience.'

'No man can entirely escape the moral blindnesses of his own time.'

'It was he, after all, who first thundered against the practice of experimenting on animals.'

'Anyway, Herbert, you are arguing from authority, which is always a weak form of argumentation.'

'With all due respect, Francis, I would hardly put your moral authority on a par with Doctor Johnson's.'

'However great a man of the past may have been, we must think for ourselves.'

'But surely not by starting from scratch, without regard for what great minds have thought before us?'

'That is not what I am suggesting. I am merely pointing out that no one's authority is absolute or exempt from examination in the light of reason. *Nullius in verba*, as our illustrious Restoration scientists put it.'

Their conversation, or sparring, had slowed their eating. Just then, Ferenc came to their table, a little more bent over than usual.

'I am sorry to interrupt, gentlemen,' he said. His Middle European accent was stronger than usual. 'There has been a terrible accident in the kitchen.'

The two men, having lived more or less event-free lives, were startled.

'No one injured, I trust?' said Herbert, approximating anxiety. He had visions of a bleeding man on a stretcher being evacuated through the restaurant, bringing lunch to an end. The two men looked at each other as if preparing for a swift and tactful, if inconvenient, departure.

'No, no, nothing like that,' said Ferenc. 'Please reassure yourselves.'

'What, then?' asked Francis.

'We have a new boy in the kitchen — Sri Lankan. He had references, but of course references can be bought or forged.'

'These days,' said Herbert, 'you are not allowed to write a bad one, in case you should upset the subject of it.'

'Yes,' said Ferenc. 'It is terrible. Anyway, the new kitchen boy muddled up the pork and the veal when it came from the market today. I am afraid that what should have been the pork is veal, and what should have been veal is pork. If you wish, I will replace the dishes...'

'I don't think that will be necessary, do you?' Herbert asked Francis.

'No, I shouldn't think so,' said Francis.

'That won't be necessary, Ferenc,' said Herbert, turning to the waiter, pleased with his own magnanimity.

'Thank you for your understanding,' said Ferenc. 'I will cancel the bill for today, you eat on the house.' He disappeared with his accustomed self-effacement.

'I suspected that there was something wrong with my ragout,' said Francis.

'You said nothing.'

'I didn't want to alarm you.'

'Why should it have alarmed me?'

'Besides, it was not at all disagreeable.'

They each resumed eating from the plate before them.

'Do you not think,' said Francis between mouthfuls, 'that the way in which pigs are raised to produce pork cheaply raises troubling ethical questions?'

'Your humanitarian concerns have migrated from calves to pigs, I see, with the main ingredient of your ragout.'

'Pigs,' said Francis, 'are highly intelligent creatures, far more so than cows and, *a fortiori*, calves. In point of self-consciousness, I believe that they are held to be the equal of dogs. They are as intelligent and as capable of affection as dogs. I trust that you wouldn't raise dogs in the way that pigs are raised.'

'A foolish consistency is the hobgoblin of little minds.'

'If inconsistency is not the refutation of an argument, or in this case of a rationalisation, it is difficult to see how anything is to be discussed. All that is left is main force.'

'No man is as consistent as he thinks he is or claims to be.'

'That does not absolve us from the duty to be as consistent as possible, otherwise we shall live in complete mental anarchy.'

'Where would literature be without inconsistency?'

'Portrayal of inconsistence and inconsistency itself are not the same thing, nor is portrayal endorsement of what is portrayed.'

'So you look forward to a world without inconsistency?'

'I think there will always be enough to satisfy anyone's desire for it. Human inconsistency will see us out.'

'A world without inconsistency would have no need of literature.'

'The purpose of life is not literature. Literature is not an end in itself.'

'What is it an end to?'

'Whatever it is that life is an end to.'

'At any rate, we have made it an end to *our* lives.'

'I don't think we should set ourselves up as models for others. A population of litterateurs would starve to death.'

'A population of anything exclusively would starve to death. I don't think we have anything to reproach ourselves with on that account.'

'Do you feel that we have lived usefully, as usefully as possible?'

'I feel that *I* have. Of course, I can't speak for you. You have had a different career.'

The two had by now eaten — absentmindedly, of course — their respective dishes, and a Hungarian dessert followed. After coffee and a *digestif*, they were ready to leave.

Although their destinations were in the same direction, they parted as soon as they left the restaurant, Herbert turning to the right and Francis to the left. Without ever saying so or making it explicit, they kept their friendship within strict limits, quarantining it as it were from the rest of their lives. In fact, their lives contained many compartments: in such a way could they keep complete catastrophe at bay. If one compartment collapsed or was destroyed, there remained the others, and so nothing could overwhelm them.

They agreed, as usual, to meet in a month's time.

Herbert was on time, but Francis was a little late. He arrived breathlessly, as if he had been hurrying.

'I do apologise for my unpunctuality,' he said, as if Herbert had not been a friend of over fifty years, 'but there was an accident on the Underground — if you can call suicide an accident.' Francis settled on his chair. 'Except metaphorically, of course.'

'A weak metaphor, usually loosely applied, by sports commentators, for example.'

'Unlike you, apparently, I wouldn't know about that,' said Francis. 'Anyway, someone threw himself in front of a train in Leicester Square.'

'I don't much care for Leicester Square myself,' said Herbert, 'but that is going a little far, surely?'

'Have you noticed how, when someone throws himself under a train, the passengers divide into two groups?'

'I can't say that I have,' said Herbert. 'Perhaps I ought to travel on the Underground more often.'

'Yes, they divide into those who want to get a closer look and those who complain about the delay and wonder why the suicide couldn't have chosen a different time and place.'

'Into which of the two categories do you fall?' asked Herbert.

'I observe.'

'That makes three categories, then.'

'You are too precise, Herbert,' said Francis. 'I was speaking *grosso modo*.'

'That is the difference between scholarship and journalism,' said Herbert.

'And why scholarship often slips into pedantry.'

'And journalism into inaccuracy.'

They chose from the menu before deciding, or at least lamenting, the state of the world.

Towards the end of their main course, Herbert said, 'I suppose you saw Smith's latest review in the *TLS*.'

Smith had been a contemporary of theirs at college and had become a well-known writer.

'I glanced at it. I didn't read it thoroughly.'

'No good, of course.'

'Of course. That's why I didn't read it thoroughly. I didn't need to.'

'His success has always been a testimony to the declining standards of our time.'

'His mind was always of the most ordinary.'

'The recipe for success in an undiscriminating, not to say non-discriminating, age.'

'He never said anything that wasn't either obvious or untrue.'

'Despite which — or perhaps I should say because of which — he sells well, wins prizes and appears on television.'

'Who reads him, I wonder?'

'Housewives and commuters.'

'Do you think he would have had such a success a hundred

years ago?'

'He wouldn't even have been published.'

'Bad novels were at least well-written when we were growing up.'

'Edgar Wallace left school when he was twelve, but he wrote better than university graduates today.'

'Not a high hurdle.'

'But Smith has no excuse for his atrocious style. He ought to know better. Most of our generation do.'

'He can't even punctuate properly.'

'That, surely, is his editor's fault?'

'True, but the manuscripts of educated persons should not require such editing. They should contain no such errors in the first place.'

'There have been great writers who were notoriously bad at spelling.'

'Punctuation and orthography are different. The former is a matter of judgment, the latter of memory.'

'Judgment surely cannot operate without memory.'

'No doubt, but there is still a difference, the one being more primitive that the other, and the more easily reparable.'

'No doubt you noticed the egregious punctation in the middle of the article. It stood out like a lighthouse.'

'Remind me.'

'Smith placed the exclamation mark after instead of before the closure of the quotation marks, as he should have done and as the sense demanded.'

'I am not quite with you there.'

'Surely the matter is hardly one of opinion, it is a straightforward question of what is correct or incorrect.'

'Whether the exclamation mark should have been inside or outside the quotation marks surely depends on the meaning the author wished to convey?'

'How so?'

'Well, if the exclamation mark were inside the quotation marks, it would mean that the speaker, as reported by the author, were exclaiming, whereas if the mark were outside, it would be the author who was exclaiming about what the speaker had said.'

'Surely it was clear from the context which it was?'

'The two positions are different in meaning or feeling-tone, I grant you that. But who are we to say which was in Smith's mind when he wrote as he did?'

'His meaning was clear, just badly-expressed.'

'Meaning is never clear. That is why critics are needed.'

'But had the exclamation mark been rightly placed, that is to say after the closure, the meaning would have been perfectly clear, and as it stands, it is not. It is ambiguous in the worst sense.'

'You remember your *Rasselas*, of course?'

'What are you driving at?'

'Inconsistencies, answered Imlac, cannot both be right, but imputed to man, they may both be true.'

'And so?'

'The mere fact that a certain reading introduces inconsistencies into Smith's article cannot prove that it is wrong, especially when you remember that Smith is hardly the sharpest knife in the box.'

'I think you are being sophistical.'

'On the contrary, there is an important point at issue. You

are abandoning yourself to the intentional fallacy, that the author's intention can be known, deciding on its basis a point of punctuation.'

'The intentional fallacy is not a fallacy. I am inclined to call it the intentional fallacy fallacy. An author, after all, must intend a meaning in what he writes, unless he is indulging in automatic writing.'

'That is only half-true. Many a writer, in my opinion, hopes that the reader will supply a meaning to the words he commits to paper, preferably, of course, a profound one. But more importantly, we can never know what the author's intentions were, and a question that can never be answered is an idle one.'

'That is so in some cases, no doubt. But often there is collateral evidence, letters, memoirs and the like.'

'They are rarely explicit and may not in any case be truthful. Moreover, a man may — in fact, often does — mistake his intentions.'

'I think you are arguing for the sake of it,' said Herbert, who was growing exasperated.

'What other reason is there for doing so?' asked Francis.

'To find the truth!' replied Herbert, his tone somewhat mounted. He put down the glass which he had been holding, suspended between the table and his mouth, with an audible firmness, almost a crash.

Francis in his turn was irritated.

'You were always a seeker after truth, weren't you, Herbert?' he said. 'Provided it was to be found in the archives and disturbed nobody.'

'And for you, approximation was always enough, wasn't it,

Francis? It was always more important to be interesting or controversial than to serve the truth.'

'Don't be ridiculous, Herbert. You make *The Lettered World* sound like a scandal sheet.'

'And wasn't it?' Herbert was agitated now. 'It was you who published the forged letters to prove that George Eliot had an affair with Dickens.'

'A mistake, admittedly,' said Francis. 'But we had taken advice — from academics, be it remembered.'

'From Halliwell. Everyone knew that he was past it, if he was ever up to it. He was senile and could hardly see.'

'You cannot deny his scholarship.'

'I can and I do. You chose him because he was pliable, and you wanted to publish. You needed to revive the circulation.'

Francis picked up a knife and brought it down on a plate with a clatter.

'That is where the intentional fallacy gets you!' he said. 'Accusing your oldest friend almost of corruption! Ascribing the worst of motives to everyone!'

'You're losing your temper because you know that what I say is true.'

'So you know my motives now better than I know them myself, do you? You, who have spent your life among the dust and dead silverfish of archives which no one has ever examined before because they were too obscure to have interested anyone with half a life to live. How would you know anyone's motives, you who have never met anyone or done anything?'

'And you?' said Herbert, standing up. 'Your precious *Lettered World*, which you spent your life guiding gently to bankruptcy, well-merited and long overdue I should add, won't it survive only in archives of the type that you so disparage and that no one will consult — that is, if anyone bothers to preserve it at all, which these days seems unlikely.'

Herbert prepared to leave.

'I suppose you're planning to leave without paying your share of the bill under guise of righteous agitation,' said Francis. 'Despite your inflated pension.'

And despite the plush, despite the semi-isolation of their near-cubicle, their dispute could now be heard in all the restaurant. The customers put down their knives and forks to listen.

Francis was now standing too. Herbert's face was contorted by hatred.

'How dare you say such a thing?' he said. 'I suppose you've forgotten how I helped you when we were students and your girlfriend needed an illegal abortion?'

Ferenc had appeared to find out what was going on, but too late. With a movement of his arm, Francis swept the plates and cutlery off the table, the tablecloth following more slowly. A vase of flowers smashed into shards.

'Blimey!' exclaimed Ferenc, forgetting his Central European origins for a moment and reverting to those of his native Shoreditch.

There were no more monthly meetings between Herbert and Francis.

PARTING OF THE WATERS

Mrs Bennett was allergic to the Twentieth Century. All its products made her ill except for a very select few, difficult to come by and expensive. In particular, there was only one kind of water that she could tolerate, all others causing an immediate reaction. It was bottled in Bavaria and came from a single source. It was hardly known outside Bavaria and rarely exported. Mrs Bennett not only drank it but bathed in it.

This was all the more remarkable (and difficult) because she lived in Africa, where I was for a time her neighbour, if someone living three miles away can be called a neighbour. She, her husband and I were the only white people in an area the size of a small European country, and we were thrown much upon each other's company.

The countryside was of rolling hills, intensely green, of sufficient elevation to mitigate the heat of the tropical latitude. It was given to violent thunderstorms: I have never known anywhere where so many people were stuck by lightning. This naturally reinforced the superstitions of the local people. For them, nothing happened except by design. Someone somewhere must have willed whatever happened, and since what happened was often disastrous, their world was full of malevolent beings, human and otherwise. A lightning strike that killed naturally caused the search for the witch or wizard who had done it, although witchcraft had been officially abolished and forbidden by the government. More than one man, or more usually woman, had been expelled from the village for having killed a fellow-villager by lightning. The women expelled were mainly widows, for it was only from them that property could be appropriated after expulsion. As the Chinese say, a crisis is also an opportunity.

Mr Bennett was the manager of a tea plantation. It had fallen into desuetude after the country's independence, but after it was re-sold (very cheaply) to the company from which it had been nationalised twenty years previously, Mr Bennett had been sent out to restore it to its previous condition, if not to better it. He was a professional expatriate who had worked all his life in foreign and mostly remote climes, so that he was now a foreigner everywhere, not least at home. It was his way, perhaps, of disengaging himself from the emotions, often distressing, of strong attachment to any one place: for it is only with such attachment that distress at the manifest faults of any place affect you deeply.

He was, I think, religious, but in a quiet and unobtrusive manner. He felt no obligation to convert others to his faith, of which I was, naturally, glad; but nevertheless, his discretion in the matter seemed a little odd, even contradictory, to me. I thought that if I had believed that I had known the secret of eternal life, one that was perfect and without misery (though I couldn't imagine what such a life might be), I could hardly have shut up about it. Keeping such a secret to oneself, after all, especially as the alternative to the perfect life was eternal torment, would hardly be the decent thing to do.

He was intelligent but not intellectual. In his time, he had been a sportsman, but that time was past. He would have hunted had there been much to hunt, but the increase in the population had depleted the larger local fauna. Gone were the days when, after nightfall, the people huddled in their huts for fear of leopard, an animal that, like Man, killed for the pleasure of it. Now there was only what was called *bushmeat* left, small animals that, when caught, were hung unskinned for sale in the local butcher's, a wooden stall in one of the larger villages: animals with little meat on them but nevertheless a treat for the better-off peasants. Very occasionally, it is true, a large animal such as an elephant, would stray from the plains that were not far away, but this was because it was old and ill and soon to die, usually pathetic examples of their species. Occasionally also there were reports of leopard in search of dogs or other easy prey, causing much excitement, as did the capture of a python with a goat inside, the snake being publicly executed and eaten. But the animals most in evidence were the zebu cattle, usually skeletal, whose ownership was more for prestige than economic advantage.

Mr Bennett was an enlightened manager. His enlightenment was a consequence of his underlying kindness. He was not of the school that drove employees into the ground in the belief that ruthlessness was realism and exaction was efficiency. He thought that decent treatment was the way to obtain the best from his workers, even if their best was sometimes not all that he could have desired. He refurbished the little clinic for the workers and their families that had fallen into abeyance and hired a competent nurse to work in it. Naturally, she purloined some of the medicaments for resale elsewhere, but to expect complete honesty from people so poor who were put in the way of temptation would have been like expecting the truth from the mouth of a politician. Like an enlightened Russian aristocrat of the second half of the Nineteenth Century, he built a little school on the estate, better than any for miles around. Of course, there were limits to what he could do — the plantation was, after all, a commercial and not a philanthropic enterprise — but still he was regarded locally as a benevolent semi-deity. He had to be careful also not to become too popular: the ruling party wouldn't have liked that.

In circumstances such as were then mine, one quickly achieves intimacy with neighbours that might otherwise have taken years to achieve, if achieved at all. The fact that such intimacy is likely to end at the most in a few years makes it all the more intense. It is easy to be intimate with someone whom you will never subsequently meet.

Perhaps one of the reasons that Mr Bennett was so happy at work was that he was so unhappy at home. Mrs Bennett was very demanding in a quiet but inexorable way. Her putative ill-health gave her a lever with which, if she could not quite lift the world, she could control her husband. She had only to hint at a symptom (which she did often) for his brow to become furrowed by consternation. What inner state of mind these outward expressions corresponded to I cannot say for certain, but it seemed to me that there was something tired and ritualistic about them. Mrs Bennett's symptoms were always vague, neither requiring nor susceptible to specific treatment, except peace and quiet and being waited upon.

I visited the Bennetts often. On these occasions, Mrs Bennett had nothing of the chronic invalid about her. Although there were many things that she could not eat, or said that she could not eat, her appetite was good for those things 'allowed' her, or that she allowed herself. She even permitted herself a glass of wine — provided that it came from the one vineyard in the world whose product did not cause her an immediate and crushing headache, along with other symptoms both describable and indescribable. The wine, if I remember, was a Corbières called *L'Extrême de Castelmaure*. The label, I must say, was rather splendid, and I could not help but wonder whether it was the label that decided Mrs Bennett in its favour. I confess that I sometimes thought of secretly substituting some other wine for it in her glass, but this would not only have been an adolescent prank unworthy of the adult that I then was, but it might have backfired nastily. When a person has had the same wine every day for several years, he or she would easily be able to distinguish it from another. The experiment therefore would not have worked if its purpose were to expose the absurdity of Mrs Bennett's supposed sensitivity to all other wines: sensitivity in the physiological sense or not, she would have had no difficulty in having, or at least reporting, the symptoms that all other wines allegedly produced in her. And if another wine had been substituted for hers, the person who did it could only have been me. I did not want to lose my only social contacts in so isolated a place.

There were other objections to my silly projected prank, of course. By what right does one interfere with the equilibrium of other people's lives? The reality or otherwise of Mrs Bennett's sensitivities was not the most important question about them. Man does not live by truth alone.

So I kept my silence. It was clear to me that a supply of a single vineyard wine did not appear in the middle of Africa spontaneously, indeed without a great deal of effort on somebody's part — Mr Bennett's, obviously. The very thought of the difficulties involved was enough to cause me anxiety on his behalf. The problems in which it must have involved him rose in my mind like midges in the Scottish heather.

The capital, through which the wine would have to have been imported, was nine hundred miles away by laterite road or track that hardened into bone-shaking ridges in the dry season and became a river of mud in the wet. The journey was not one best-suited to the transport of bottles, however carefully packed. And then there was the problem of theft, both private and by officialdom. For every bottle that arrived at the plantation, two had to be imported.

First the problem of passage through customs had to be solved. That took at least two crates as a bribe; without it, the import duty doubled and other obstacles in the way of release from the bonded warehouse were found. Naturally, bribery went against Mr Bennett's grain, but there was nothing for it if Mrs Bennett was to have her wine. Mr Bennett, not much of a drinker, would have contented himself with the local *Hippo* brand beer, whose supply and content were both inconstant, and which was notorious for causing a hangover without first having caused drunkenness. Mr Bennett had never succumbed to the occupational hazard of isolated residence in the tropics, namely heavy drinking.

Further up the supply chain, as it were, was the problem of securing enough of the wine in the first place. It was far from easy to come by and necessitated a search in France itself.

But the problem of the wine was as nothing compared with that of the water. The particular type was produced in sufficient quantities hardly to satisfy the local demand and was therefore never exported. Often, I wanted to ask Mr Bennett how it was that his wife had discovered it and come to the conclusion that it was the only water she could tolerate, but I never had the courage, or the insensitivity, to do so. I always kept my counsel and never said anything that could have been interpreted as scepticism with regard to his wife's condition — or conduct. I let him suppose that I thought of her condition as a brute fact of nature.

As Mrs Bennett had not only to drink this water but bathe in it, very large quantities of it were required, indeed at least two containers-full a year. The expense both in time and money to secure such a supply must have been formidable: I calculated that not a small proportion of Mr Bennett's income must have been taken up by it, and practically all his time on leave from the plantation. It is often that the absurdity of a situation is obvious to everyone except those who are in it, the inability to see a situation for what it is having nothing to do with intelligence.

Sometimes I would go to the Bennetts for dinner, and occasionally Mr Bennett would come to me for a drink and a chat. Mrs Bennett never came to visit, not only because mine was a bachelor establishment (my cook, Moses, was very good considering the lack of available ingredients), or because she could not reasonably impose her dietary restrictions on me, but because she travelled as little as possible in motor vehicle, her reaction to them, or against them (as she put it), exhausting her for a week afterwards. She totted up the number of hours she spent in vehicles and allowed herself no more than fifty in any six months. Even the short ride of three miles made her ill; nasty, smelly things, she called motor vehicles, and I couldn't help agreeing with her. Besides, she was not the kind of woman who brooked contradiction, however implicit; she spoke in tablets of stone. Conversation with her husband was more fun when she was not around.

I don't mean to say that she was altogether unamusing to be with. Once she was distracted from her medical complaints, admittedly not easy to do, she had stories to tell — mainly about the many servants she had had in her life as an expatriate, including in one or two countries engulfed by civil war. She was actually tougher than her allergies might suggest.

Or perhaps more ruthless. Sometimes Mr Bennett would have a special dispensation, an *exeat* I suppose you could call it, to spend an evening with me at my bungalow. During these evenings, he recounted what could have been a chapter in his autobiography. But it took him a long time to come to the real subject on his mind, his marriage.

He had married young, after a passionate romance. It was difficult to imagine this bronzed and weather-beaten man, apparently so balanced, as a passionate lover, but such he had been, or said that he had been. His wife's social origins were rather more elevated than his own, her father having been a major-general and his a mere manager on the railways: whose trains in those days, moreover, rarely ran to time, certainly not as punctually as they would have done under the major-general's direction. At first, the latter had been opposed to their marriage, on the universally true parental objection that she could have done better, that is to say better than a recent graduate of an agricultural college, as Mr Bennett then was; but eventually the major-general was forced to admit that he had certain sterling qualities of almost military strength and was reconciled to the alliance.

Soon after their marriage, his wife displayed the characteristic that she had displayed ever since, namely a fierce jealousy. It had come to him as a complete surprise. There had been no cause for it, that is to say none in his behaviour; her jealousy was a quirk of character and if you analysed it further, by saying that it was a manifestation of underlying lack of confidence or sense of inferiority, you would only have pushed the need for an explanation one stage back. There was thus no point in speculating as to *why* Mrs Bennett was jealous: it was best just to accept it as a fact and make one's accommodation with it.

Apart from a spirit of adventure and a natural taste for self-sufficiency and social isolation, Mr Bennett had found by experience that posts such as his present one were the least provocative of her jealousy. All the same, he had to live his life according to a timetable laid down each day so that his wife would know, at least in theory, where he was at any time of that day. This, of course, was long before the advent of the mobile telephone, which has both provoked and inflamed jealousy, proving suspicions more often than allaying them.

One of the benefits of expatriation in poor countries is the availability, and affordability, of servants. Those who could afford none at home take on an entire staff: housemaids, gardeners, cooks, drivers. It is astonishing how quickly that common scourge of previous eras, the servant problem, raises its head among people who, far from being grateful for the relief from household chores, contrive to feel themselves martyrised by those who relieve them of those chores. The fact is that no servant is perfect, especially in Africa, where strange rituals are imposed on him, rituals that have no intrinsic meeting as far he is concerned other than the propitiation of those who commanded them. There were still a few old retainers in the country who remembered the rituals of the past, such as the ironing of newspapers, from having performed them in their youth; such as these were rare, however, though I discovered one who was still working in his nineties. Our region, however, had always been remote, and the servants there had to be trained from scratch, with the natural consequences of a combination of inexperience and incomprehension.

The problem was particularly severe in Mrs Bennett's case because she had a peculiar criterion of selection of female servants: she wanted them as ugly as possible, preferably with some deformed feature from which one averted one's gaze, and none too young either. It was not from a special feeling for the unfortunate that she selected her female servants thus (though I think she wished the unfortunate no harm either), but to ensure that her husband was not put in the way of temptation. As far as I could tell, she succeeded in this; and while no man's word as to his fidelity can be taken entirely on trust, I believed Mr Bennett when he said that he had never wandered.

I was naturally curious about the origin of his wife's illness, if that is what it was. It seemed evident to me that it was largely, if not entirely, psychological in origin. No one could be truly allergic to as much as she claimed to be and survive. It was surely no coincidence that those things that she allowed herself were both difficult to find and expensive. It was by this means that she kept her husband on a tight rein, though I am not sure that he realised it.

When, on his leave from the country, he was not seeking out Bavarian water and a single French vintage, he was taking his wife from doctor to doctor in search of a cure. Naturally, all the doctors differed in their diagnoses, according to their medical specialities and personal enthusiasms. To the nephrologist, everything is a kidney. The Bennetts went from specialist to specialist, like would-be refugees applying to embassy after embassy trying desperately to get a visa, in this case for refuge in the promised land of health. I don't say that the various doctors were outright dishonest in holding out hope by their suggestion that just one more expensive test or investigation would make all clear, but the fact is that they must have derived a considerable income from Mr and Mrs Bennett. But I suppose that hope, even in its falsest guise, is better than despair. Who can live without illusion?

Did either of them ever realise the futility of their search? I doubt it; perhaps in any case futility is the wrong word. The search was not without meaning, even if what was sought was not to be found. It did not keep them happy, but it kept them stable, which after a certain stage in life is perhaps the more important.

I was by then old enough and mature enough to keep my opinion or analysis of the situation to myself. Mr Bennett would, on his visits, describe his wife's latest access of ill-health, caused allegedly by something unique to the twentieth century, perhaps something packaged in plastic which leached chemicals, or some comestible that had undergone industrial transformation. She would retire to her bed for two or three days at a time, with the implication that Mr Bennett was being slightly insensitive by continuing to enjoy apparent good health.

For the most part, Mr Bennett was descriptive rather than complaining: he recounted his marital travails with detachment and sometimes with irony. Then he would talk about something else, an event on the tea plantation, for example. There was never any shortage of such events. Sometimes it would be a conflict between members of two tribes who would attack each other with sticks; sometimes it would be an outbreak of dysentery or religious fervour.

'One day,' I said, 'you'll be able to write a book.'

To my surprise, this rather stolid and unimaginative man replied that he had thought of it. He said that it would occupy him in his retirement. I took him to mean that writing his memoirs would be for him a means of keeping boredom at bay rather than a way of enlightening the world or of obtaining literary glory.

He came to me one day in an unaccustomed state of agitation.

'What's wrong?' I asked.

'My wife,' he said. 'She's taken it into her head to get rid of all the bedclothes, curtains and soft furnishings.'

I should mention that their bungalow in that remote part of Africa was remarkably chintzy in its décor, a bit like 1950s Surrey planted in the Ngozi hills.

For the first time, I saw Mr Bennett exasperated.

'Do you have any idea what it will cost to replace them?' he asked.

Of course, I had no idea except that it would be a lot.

'What is her reason?' I asked.

'She read that the dyes used years ago contained scores of allergens. That explains why she's feeling so ill.'

'But she always feels ill.'

'Not like she's felt ever since we had these fabrics.'

Did he believe it? I could detect no expression of irony or scepticism on his face.

'So you are going to change them all?'

'I have no choice. We have to try everything.'

'I don't know how you've put up with it all these years.' It slipped out despite myself.

'What do you mean?'

I shouldn't have started this thread of conversation, but it would have appeared unnatural to change the subject.

'I couldn't have put up with it,' I said. 'If it had been me, I would have left.' I almost added, 'Long ago.'

'When I married her,' he said a little stiffly, 'I made a promise, for richer and poorer, in sickness and in health. I meant it.'

This was not so much a reproach as a statement of fact. He was the kind of man for whom breaking a promise would be unthinkable. Was this foolishness, stupidity, uprightness or heroism?

'Oh, of course,' I said, as if, in his place, I would have behaved no differently. 'You have no choice.'

'Nor want one.'

I now changed the subject.

'I hear they have armyworm in Ndala,' I said.

Armyworm was a kind of caterpillar that suddenly exploded in population and marched in wide columns across the land, consuming all vegetation in their path.

'Many years ago,' said Mr Bennett, 'I was in Northern Rhodesia as it then was, Zambia now. We set up a cricket match for all the Britons in the district. They came from miles around, a whole day's journey, but the makeshift pitch was in the path of the *okalombo*, as the locals called the armyworm. I think this must have been the only cricket match ever abandoned because of the arrival of armyworm. They stripped the land bare.'

'Will they come here?' I asked.

'No,' he replied, 'they don't like the elevation, and they don't eat tea.'

Nevertheless, Mr Bennett was worried because he bought maize, the staple food of his workers, from the very area which armyworm threatened to devastate. Being a man of prevision, he had already stored enough in reserve to meet any shortfall, but the local politicians might force him to disgorge his reserve. I suspect that the complexity of his responsibilities came as a relief to him.

Sometime later, during one of his visits, I noticed that he looked unwell. I guessed at once that there was something seriously wrong with him, though I was unable to formulate exactly how I sensed it: like one of those dogs, perhaps, that knows when its master is about to have an epileptic fit. When I asked him what was wrong, he replied almost angrily (which was most unlike him) that nothing was wrong, that he had never felt better in his life. Indeed, he reacted indignantly, like one accused of a crime of which he knew himself to be innocent — or guilty.

But in subsequent weeks there was no disguising his decline. His flesh melted away and his face became gaunt. His step became that of an old man. There was a yellowish tinge to his complexion. No man, I should imagine, was less inclined than he to worry over his health, but even he could not deny that there was something seriously wrong.

'I'm going to the capital,' he said. 'They have at least some medical facilities there.'

I knew better than to ask him for more details. He found the whole business of mortal illness faintly embarrassing, and certainly not a proper subject of conversation, especially with regard to himself.

'At least the road will not be too bad in this season,' he said, as if that were some kind of consolation for his illness.

He was away for about two weeks, and he returned in an even worse condition than at his departure.

'There's no hope for me, old boy,' he said when he returned and I saw him for the first time. 'I'm done for.'

Apparently, he had an aggressive cancer that was now consuming him and that had spread everywhere. They told him that if he returned to Europe, he could have treatment that might (or might not) prolong his life by six months, but it seemed like a bad bargain to him; and it seemed to me that he was right. The treatment would weaken him further and give him horrible side-effects for at least three of the extra six months (if that), and it might even kill him.

'They say that without it I have another three or four months,' he said.

'I'm very sorry,' I said, my mouth drying out with the banality of my words in the face of the most important fact of anyone's existence.

'It can't be helped,' he said. 'What cannot be cured must be endured. It comes to us all, and I've had a good life.'

What would have been clichés in the mouth of a man in flourishing health seemed heroic in that of a man with a countable number of days to live.

I asked whether there was anything I could do to help, without knowing what it might be. But his wife, I said, was not well, and therefore in no condition to nurse him.

'Thank you very much,' said Mr Bennett. 'But she is really managing very well.'

'Do you not think of returning home?' I asked.

'What for?' he said. 'There's no medical reason. I've been away so long that here is more home to me than there. They can bury me here and it will save on funeral expenses which I gather are now extortionate.'

From then on, I visited him often in his bungalow. It was obvious to him that I was doing so because I knew that he was not long for this world. By now, he had retired to his bed, hardly able to walk more than a few paces without heroic effort. The drawback of frequenting a man in the throes of death is that you will always remember him on his deathbed, that scene expunging from your memory all others; but the drawback of not doing so is perpetual regret that you did not do your duty merely to avoid embarrassment, and that now it is too late to make reparation.

Of course, by comparison with dying itself, the discomfort of visiting the dying is very slight, and I did my duty. Mr Bennett was stoical, which made it easier. He did not indulge in any false hopes of recovery, but neither did he speak of his imminent dissolution. He tried to speak as if my visits were a source of normal social enjoyment. He continued to express an interest in my own petty affairs and steered clear of the deeper mysteries of human existence such as one might have expected of someone about to enter the bourne from which no traveller returns.

The most remarkable effect of his grave illness was that on his wife. No woman could have been more selflessly devoted to a husband's needs than she as he became less and less able to do anything for himself. Her own illnesses, her allergies, her sensitivities, vanished, so to speak, into thin air. Suddenly she no longer felt unwell if she came into contact with any water other than her Bavarian bottled variety. The ordinary rough soap of the country no longer caused a reaction that forced her to retire to bed for a few days on the slightest contact with it. In short, she returned not only to normality but to rude good health.

Perhaps most surprising of all was the tenderness she now showed towards her husband. I had never heard any term of endearment pass between them before, but now she did not so much as mop his brow without uttering something like *my darling*. It was as if, suddenly realising what she was about to lose, she realised what she had had.

Mr Bennett's decline was inexorable. Mrs Bennett sent for

her son, of whom I had never heard either of them speak. Apparently, he was a very successful man, at least as success is commonly understood. Communication with Europe from such a remote part in Africa in those days was slow, hazardous and uncertain: even in the capital, the telephones stopped working when it rained, admittedly always in downpours. But Mrs Bennett sent a 'boy', as male servants in those days were still sometimes called by those who employed them, to the capital with a message to be transmitted home to her son. Miraculously, it worked, and just over a week later their son Justin arrived.

He was clean-cut, in his mid-thirties, exuding a confidence which one knew not to be mere bravado. He was the kind of man who could walk through a swamp and emerge with fully-laundered clothes. I had known a few people like that: alas, I am of the opposite kind. Having dressed to the best of my ability, I soon look as if I have emerged from a swamp. Justin was also the kind of man who thought that life was an organisational problem.

It was as well that he arrived when he did, for his father died a week after his arrival. He did so almost apologetically, because of the trouble it gave to others. Justin concerned himself with the burial arrangements, practical matters keeping emotion (if any) at bay. Mrs Bennett cried copiously, in a way that I should not have suspected her to be capable.

Her husband was buried on a hilltop in the plantation. His grave was marked by a wooden cross that would certainly not endure. His funeral was attended by many of the plantation workers whose regret, no doubt tinged by anxiety about who or what might come next, was genuine.

Mrs Bennett decided to leave Africa almost at once after her husband's death and return to Europe with her son, with whom she decided to live. I went to see them off at the capital's airport. I knew that I should never see them again.

The airport was as chaotic as ever, of course, despite the infrequency of the flights that landed or took off from there. The atmosphere, at least to someone who did not know the country, was of a long, drawn-out panic or hysteria, though in reality it was only disorganisation, excitement and enjoyment. We are used to airports in which arrivals and departures are so frequent that we fail to notice how astonishing a thing air transport is, as if it were nothing more than the buzzing of large flies. When there is but one flight a day, however, the extraordinary feat of a giant machine lifting into the air or coming to rest on the ground does not lose its power to astonish, all the greater to those not very far removed from subsistence.

The country was in many respects unfree, being a ridiculous political dictatorship, but in many others it was much freer, at least of bureaucratic restrictions on behaviour, than our countries. There was no control, for example, on the people who turned out at the airport to take their leave of the passengers. There was always a melee around the foot of the steps leading to the aircraft, through which the passengers had to fight their way. I joined this melee to say goodbye to Mrs Bennett.

I could see that she did not enjoy this last experience of Africa: in fact, her distaste was clear. It was not fear of violence — no crowd could have been less menacing — but, I suspect, of contamination. Her son, Justin, tried to clear a path for her like Moses parting the Red Sea, but in this he was only moderately successful. The hubbub was, as usual, deafening.

Eventually, Mrs Bennett managed to reach the steps up to the aircraft. My presence on the airport apron had long been forgotten. Justin almost pushed his mother up the steps. He followed, and a few steps up, she turned to him.

'Have you brought the water' she asked, raising her voice to make sure that he heard her.

'No,' Justin shouted back. 'They wouldn't let me, not even for money.' Actually, he had dumped it long before.

'But what am I going to drink on the flight?' Mrs Bennett wailed. 'You know I can't drink anything else.'

The Restaurant Trade

When Gwyneth Ford returned to Walport as Mrs Ahmed Bensousa, she created a sensation. Until then, she had seemed such a quiet and sensible girl, level-headed and without *histoires*, as the French say. She had trained as a nurse and had always said that her ambition was to return to her native town to look after its elderly residents. She must have had a sudden rush of blood to the head because she married her Algerian after a whirlwind holiday romance in France where she met him. She couldn't have known him for more than a week.

Tongues wagged, of course. There is nothing people like more in a small town in which nothing happens than to shake their head in sorrowful, which is to say secretly joyful, disapproval of one of its inhabitants.

'She doesn't even know who he is or where he comes from.'
'It'll end badly."
'He's an Arab. You know how they treat women. He'll lock her up.'
'He's probably got other wives at home.'
'She's a slut.'
'Have you seen him? Thin and wiry — dangerous, I would

say.'

'I bet he always carries a knife, they always do.'

'You'd have to watch your back with him, especially when he's trying to seem nice.'

'They believe in slavery.'

'I don't see what she sees in him. His skin is all sallow and leathery.'

'She's made her bed, now she'll have to lie on it.'

'Marry in haste…'

'Even a black would have been better…'

'He seems all right, though, polite and everything.'

'They always do at first, but they're treacherous. Stab you in the back while smiling at you, they will.'

'He only married her to be allowed to come here. He'll soon be off. That type always are.'

'You watch. Soon he'll bring his whole family to live here. They breed like rabbits.'

Ahmed had been a teacher of mathematics in France, mostly of pupils who did not want to learn. His English was halting but rapidly improved. Contrary to the general opinion that he came only to live on social security, he sought work, first as a teacher of mathematics (but there were no openings in Walport, and anyway his qualifications did not count), then as a private teacher of French, but there was only one person in Walport who wanted to learn it (and she was seventy and too old to retain anything from one lesson to the next).

Clearly, Ahmed would have to find a different means of support. Gwyneth's part-time work was not enough to support them. They could barely afford the rent of their small and dingy flat in an Edwardian conversion where the other tenants were deadbeat young people who had come to the seaside to idle away their days in a drug-addled haze. Luckily, they were not aggressive or violent, only useless.

Ahmed had some savings, though, and decided to use them to open a small and simple Moroccan restaurant. He had never cooked before, but he thought he could learn easily enough. He went to the nearest large city for a time and offered his labour free to a Moroccan restaurant there so that he could learn the trade. He told the owner that he wanted to open a restaurant in Walport that would offer him no competition.

He was away for three months. The gossips rejoiced at their own perspicacity.

'I knew it couldn't last.'

'They have several wives dotted about everywhere.'

'He probably discovered that she wasn't a virgin.'

But Ahmed returned and to everyone's surprise rented a premises that he started to transform into a restaurant. He and Gwyneth worked on it fourteen or fifteen hours a day. It was he who directed the work: Gwyneth followed his instructions. He installed a kitchen behind a partition, painted the walls with roughly arabesque designs, bought some mosaic-topped tables, and hired a sign-painter to paint the front. Though he was Algerian, he called the restaurant *Moroccan* because no one in Walport had heard of Algeria or knew where it was, or thought that it was dangerous, full of mad mullahs and civil wars, whereas a number of the inhabitants had been on holiday to Morocco and liked it.

At home, Ahmed taught Gwyneth how to cook North African food, as near as the local availability of ingredients permitted. By the time of the opening, Gwyneth had resigned her job as a nurse in order to help Ahmed in his enterprise. It was generally agreed that he had forced her to do so, probably by threats or violence.

'Their religion allows them to beat their wives.'

'It even requires them to.'

The day before the opening, someone had sprayed the words *Arabs out!* on the restaurant window. Gwyneth wiped them off.

'See what he makes her do.'

'They're cowards.'

'And dictators.'

They opened the restaurant at six in the evening and waited for the first customers to arrive. None did. To console Gwyneth who was almost in tears as they closed for the evening, Ahmed said it was just as he had expected.

'People don't know yet what North African food is,' he said. 'But they'll learn, and then they will like it.'

Curiosity began to drive a few brave souls into the *Marrakech*, as it was called. Most of them demanded chips with their tajine or couscous. A meal out without chips was for them unthinkable. Ahmed soon learned to oblige, though he still explained to the customers that, in North Africa, they did not eat chips. Some of the customers eventually learned to go without.

Walport was on the sea-coast; a hundred years earlier it had been almost fashionable. That was in the days when people on their holidays were content to walk up and down the promenade, listen to brass bands that played in the elaborate wrought iron bandstand and spend their evenings chatting or playing bridge. Those days were long gone: the bandstand had decayed and was now mainly used by youths in the dead of night to buy and sell cannabis or amphetamine, depending on whether they wanted to be calmed down or fired up, or both. By day it was the haunt of drunks who gathered there to consume their cans of strong beer or cider and shout nonsense at one another and passers-by, with sudden gusts of inconsequential laughter. Once, a few years before, the railing against which one of them was leaning had given way and he fell a few feet on to the ground, breaking his elbow. Luckily it was not of the arm with which he raised his drink to his lips, but nevertheless the council placed notices round the bandstand warning the public that the railings were fragile and should not be leant against.

In the summer season, trippers still came to Walport for short holidays. It was not a destination for the rich or cultivated. Indeed, it was not easy to see why anybody should come; the beach was of pebbles and difficult to walk on, besides which it was littered with plastic bottles; and the sea was generally grey and always cold. But a change is as good as a rest for the bored, and visitors drank as if they had a grudge against consciousness itself. It was not until they were in a state of inebriety that they went in search of something to eat.

That was late at night. The Marrakech was situated between a tattoo parlour — cleverly called *I Ink Therefore I Am* — and a solicitor's office that offered advice on such matters as domestic violence, protection against eviction, and compensation for accidents.

By the time of its first summer season, the Marrakech had established a clientele for somewhat better-heeled residents of the town. A few began to call Ahmed by his name; he was always polite and welcoming, and as people said on their way from the restaurant, he was a human being nevertheless, as if this were surprising. Some even went so far as to say that the Marrakech was a useful addition to or adornment of the town. As to the marriage, they were now willing to suspend judgment. Perhaps Gwyneth had not chosen as badly as they had at first thought.

The Marrakech was profitable in a small way.

The season tested Ahmed's and Gwyneth's resolve. Sometimes a party of ten or twelve would arrive just as they were closing and demand immediate service. The hilarity of the party would be menacing: it could so quickly turn to irritation and then to violence. The slightest delay in filling their order seemed to them an assault on their rights or dignity. They did not know what they were ordering, and when it arrived they would demand to know 'What's this shit?' and claim that they had never ordered it or anything like it. For some, this was an excuse not to pay, though they had eaten it. Others objected to the North African music, which was intended to create an exotic atmosphere, but such an atmosphere, unfamiliar, only inflamed their contempt. One customer threw a bottle of beer at the speaker in the upper corner, but by then Ahmed and Gwyneth had learned that it was useless to call the police. There were no police in Walport by night: they had to come from the nearest station fifteen miles away, and as they always had something more urgent to attend to, they arrived, if they arrived at all, well after the bird had flown, as it were. The first time they called the police, two fat agents of the law, a man and a woman, arrived three hours later, in badly-fitting stab-vests and the apparatus of repression dangling from them like decorations. It was a case of ten customers who had not only left without payment, laughing as they did so, but had swept everything from the tables on to the floor.

'What do you expect us to do about it?' asked the policeman.

'To find them,' said Ahmed.

'What, after all this time?' said the policeman with a derisive little laugh.

'We called you straight away,' said Gwyneth, having slowly woken up. It was now nearly three in the morning.

'We was busy,' said the policeman.

The policeman then gave Ahmed and Gwyneth a piece of avuncular advice.

'If you didn't want no trouble, you shouldn't of opened a restaurant in Walport. It's famous for trouble, is Walport. If I was you, I'd go somewhere else, more peaceful like.'

'But I thought you were supposed…'

'We can't be everywhere. There's a limit to what we can do.'

So saying, the two enforcers of the law took their leave. As they left, the policeman turned slightly and said, 'Think about what I said.'

Of course, it was only a minority of customers, even drunk ones, who left without paying or gave any trouble. In the season, Ahmed and Gwyneth now made a decent living. But they lived always in a state of tension, for though infrequent, trouble could break out at any time. Once or twice, they had had to re-open the restaurant after closure for the night because of a menacing group that banged on the windows demanding to be fed. 'This is supposed to be a f.....g restaurant, isn't it?' they demanded to know.

Nevertheless, the Marrakech had established itself, and Ahmed and Gwyneth were proud of their achievement. At first, they lived in a flat above the restaurant, but then they decided to buy a house a few streets away. One of the neighbours wouldn't speak to them at first — he didn't hold with mixed marriages — but eventually even he passed the time of day with them if he saw them in the street.

The Marrakech even prospered. They were able to redecorate it in more elaborate Moorish style with metal lanterns with multicoloured glass panels. They decorated the little passage to the lavatory with pictures of camels and casbahs.

Just when things seemed to be running smoothly — they now took drunken incidents within their stride — a new problem arose in the form of a competitor. A man called Aksil Boulifa, fair-skinned and green-eyed, arrived in Walport and together with some friends began to turn some premises a few doors away into a restaurant called *The Atlas*.

'Why does he want to open up here?' asked Gwyneth. 'There are plenty of other places without a Moroccan restaurant he could go.'

'He's a Kabyle,' said Ahmed.

'What's that?' asked Gwyneth.

She was surprised to learn that not all Algerians were Arabs, nor did they all like each other.

'Just the same as here,' said Ahmed.

They watched anxiously as The Atlas took shape. Certainly,

a lot of money was being spent on it. It was going to be a lot more luxurious than the Marrakech, which remained simple and almost rustic by comparison. Everything in the Atlas was glaring and eye-catching.

'It won't work,' said Gwyneth, trying to reassure Ahmed and herself. 'They'll have to charge too much.'

'You don't know these Kabyles,' said Ahmed. 'They're cunning. They'll want to destroy us.'

They watched Aksil Boulifa give directions to the workers. He behaved as if the Marrakech did not exist.

Soon it was time for the Atlas to open. Somehow or other, Aksil Boulifa arranged a grand opening. There was a reporter from the local newspaper and a photographer who took pictures of Aksil Boulifa with the mayor, Fred Rugle, who came in his fur-trimmed red robe and gold chain of office and cut the ribbon across the Atlas's entrance. He made a grandiloquent speech, considering that all his life he had been a school caretaker and odd-job man. He said that the Atlas was an adornment to the town and a sign of confidence in its future on the part of investors, a proof that it was emerging from the doldrums into which it had fallen when the Navy had moved out sixty-three years ago. On the contrary, it was now go ahead, spearheading a drive to diversity.

'I wonder how much they paid him to say that?' asked Gwyneth when she read the account in the *East Minstshire Gazette*. The article was headlined *Walport to have taste of Eastern luxury*.

It was only to be expected that customers should try the Atlas out of curiosity. For a week or two after the opening, the Marrakech had hardly any business. Then most, but not all, of the regulars drifted back; but there was no disguising the fact that business was down from its not very elevated peak. And though the passing trade of the drunken trippers was nerve-wracking and far from pleasing, its division by two was a serious blow to the Marrakech's prosperity. Because of the Atlas, Ahmed and Gwyneth were back to scraping by.

Aksil Boulifa studiously avoided them.

'Don't you think we should introduce ourselves to him?' asked Gwyneth. 'After all, he *is* your fellow-countryman.'

'It would do no good. It would make him angry.'

'Why?'

'We come from the same country, but we are not fellow-countrymen.'

One day, however, Aksil Boulifa knocked on the door of the Marrakech just as they were preparing to open for the evening. He smiled as though they were old friends united after a long absence.

'I am Aksil Boulifa,' he said, after having called the blessings of God down upon them, introducing himself as if they might have mistaken him for someone else. 'I am your neighbour, the owner of the Atlas.'

Ahmed bowed slightly, his right hand over his heart.

'Welcome,' he said.

They spoke in English for Gwyneth's sake, though Aksil did not really approve of the marriage. Ahmed treated his wife too much as an equal for his taste, which was how things fell apart.

At first, they discussed things of mutual interest such as the behaviour of their customers.

'They are barbarians,' said Aksil.

'Not all of them,' said Ahmed.

'Not all, but most.'

'The women are the worst.'

Sometimes the women held hen parties at which they would not so much cackle as scream. Why was it that they couldn't talk but seemed to have to screech? Was something funnier just because the laughter shook the interior of the restaurant? And the women could turn just as vicious as the men. Hilarity could soon turn into a fight: because of some casual or stupid remark, the women might start to insult one another and two of them would then roll on the floor, scratching and biting at each other, and pulling each other's hair. More than once, Ahmed had had to separate two such women, which was like trying to separate two cats fighting in a black bag. Once he had succeeded, they turned on him, as if the fight had been his fault and he were responsible for the bloody scratches on their faces.

Having exhausted their repertoire of stories about the evils of their customers, Aksil Boulifa changed the subject. He looked grave.

'Walport is very small,' he said.

This was undeniable.

'I do not think there is room for two restaurants.'

Ahmed pointed out that it had been Aksil's decision, not his, to open a second, with the implication that, if there was not enough business to go round, it was his fault. Aksil ignored this slur.

'It would be better if there was only one,' he said.

This, too, was undeniable: but the question was, which of the two restaurant was surplus to the market.

'I have invested a lot of money in the Atlas,' said Aksil.

'That was your decision,' interposed Gwyneth, who had heard the rumour that Aksil ran his establishment to launder money and deal in drugs. Certainly, shady characters seemed to gather there, young men with gold front teeth and BMWs. But Aksil was the kind of man who would want even a front organisation (if that is what it was) to be profitable.

'I am prepared to make you an offer,' he said.

'An offer for what?'

'An offer for you to close down the Marrakech. I will give you ten thousand pounds.'

'But we don't want to close down the Marrakech,' said Gwyneth. 'We built it up ourselves.'

'Fifteen thousand,' said Aksil.

'We don't want to close it at any price,' said Gwyneth.

Aksil made a gesture towards Ahmed to indicate that it was he, not his wife, who must decide.

'We were here first,' said Ahmed. 'We don't want to leave.'

Aksil stood up to go. They had been sitting round a table. Gwyneth had brought mint tea. Aksil looked grim. He clenched his jaw and narrowed his eyes.

'Think about it,' he said. 'I will go to twenty thousand pounds but no more. If you don't accept my offer...'

'What?' said Ahmed, but Aksil affected not to hear.

'I will come again in a week,' he said, as he left.

When he had gone. Gwyneth told Ahmed that she didn't like the look of Aksil. He was menacing.

'What can he do?' said Ahmed. 'These Kabyles, they are all mouth.'

Gwyneth was not so sure. She awaited his return visit with trepidation.

Aksil duly returned as he said that he would. He turned down Gwyneth's offer of tea, saying that he had not much time. This was ominous. He said that he had to prepare for the evening opening though they knew that this was not true because, unlike them, he had staff, two dubious characters one of whom looked like a professional poisoner.

'Have you thought about my offer?' he said.

'Yes,' said Ahmed. 'We've decided to stay.'

Gwyneth thought it best to be emollient.

'You see, I was born here,' she said. 'My parents live here. Apart from when I went to college, I have lived here all my life. We started this restaurant ourselves. I'm sure you'll understand, Mr Boulifa, why we want to stay.'

Mr Boulifa did not appear to understand, or even to try to understand. He had not even sat down, so much in a hurry was he, or claimed by his manner to be. As Gwyneth spoke, he drummed his fingers on the table.

'So that's your decision,' he said.

'Yes,' said Ahmed.

'We thank you for your offer,' said Gwyneth, alarmed by the look on Mr Boulifa's face.

'You'll regret it,' he said.

When he had gone, Gwyneth told Ahmed that she was frightened by what Mr Boulifa might do. He had looked not only angry but vicious and determined. Ahmed tried to be reassuring, but it is hard to reassure convincingly when you are not convinced yourself.

'What can he do?' said Ahmed. 'Nothing.'

Their days were filled with apprehension, all the worse because they did not know where or how the blow would fall, or what it would be. Then, a few days later, a regular customer drew Ahmed aside as he left. He had a conspiratorial air, as people often do when they want to be seen to convey secrets.

'Have you seen what's been written about you on the *Visit Walport* site?' he asked Ahmed.

'No, what?'

'You should look. I don't want to repeat it.'

Ahmed told Gwyneth to look; she was better at that kind of thing.

Visit Walport vaunted the attractions of the town, and a clever photographer had even managed to make some of its streets look quaint and attractive. There was a section called *Feeling peckish?* which listed all the town's restaurants and cafés and permitted customers to leave their comments.

The difference between what was said about the Marrakech and the Atlas was startling. In the Atlas, the food was delicious and the atmosphere warm and welcoming. Everyone wanted to return as soon as possible. The Marrakech, by contrast, was dirty, the food was disgusting, the service was slow and rude, and the public was advised by many customers to avoid the place at all costs. It was better to go hungry than to eat there. Some of the comments were sarcastic: 'Brings North African standards of hygiene to Walport', 'or 'The meat they serve must have been the leftovers from a flyblown souk imported by the Marrakech'. Another said that the restaurant claimed to be Moroccan, but its owner was Algerian, and its food had nothing to do with Morocco.

It was obvious that Aksil Boulifa was behind all this commentary. It was true that Ahmed was Algerian, but so was Aksil Boulifa, besides which the cuisine of the two countries was practically identical, and the deception, if there was one, was trivial. The other accusations were preposterous.

The trouble was that they were effective. Few visitors would patronise the Marrakech: they avoided it, while the Atlas was often full, with people waiting for a place. The derogatory comments on the site were more numerous than the customers, in fact, and whoever wrote them entered a kind of competition as to the worst insult. As the *Visit Walport* site was run by the council, Ahmed and Gwyneth decided to ask it to halt the unjustified abuse.

Although the council had few powers and relatively little to do, its offices were in Walport's one rather grand Georgian house, whose interior had, of course, been eviscerated to make room for offices and fluorescent lighting, as well as storerooms for cardboard cartons. The town clerk, a nervous little man whose left eye had a tic so that it seemed to wink all the time, though with no concomitant amusement, and who was obsequious to those above him (not many in Walport) and bullying to those below, agreed to meet them only at their third attempt. He gave the impression that he was extremely busy and that to be allowed to see him was an extraordinary concession on his part.

'What can I do for you?' he asked abruptly, as if words were taxpayers' money that it was his duty to spend wisely. His parsimony did not extend to the decoration of his office, which had striped silk curtains.

First, they explained who they were.

'Yes, I know,' he said, as if it were an insult to suggest that he didn't. 'Well?'

They explained that they had come about the website and

the insults posted on it.

'Can you do something about it?' asked Gwyneth.

'I'm the town clerk, not the town censor,' he replied. 'I can't tell people what to write.'

'But what they write is untrue.'

'According to you.'

'Look at what they say about us.'

There was a computer on the town clerk's desk, and he called up the *Visit Walport* website. He scrolled down it.

'It says here that the Marrakech is a Morocccan restaurant.'

'That's right.'

'But you're Algerian, aren't you?' he said, turning to Ahmed.

'Yes, but Algeria and Morocco are almost the same. Their food is identical, in fact.'

'But people wouldn't go to an Algerian restaurant,' said Gwyneth.

'That's why we call it the Marrakech,' said Ahmed.

'You admit it's a lie, then?'

'There are plenty of so-called Turkish restaurants that sell pizza,' said Gwyneth.

'But they don't call the pizza Turkish. Besides,' said the town clerk, turning again to Ahmed, 'I don't know whether you've heard the English proverb, two wrongs don't make a right?'

'But look at what else they say,' said Gwyneth, now a little plaintively.

It was too late. The town clerk had switched off his computer with a flourish of finality. He stood, having a habit of drawing himself up as if it added cubits to his height.

'There is nothing more I can do,' he said, 'and I'm afraid I'm very busy.'

Ahmed and Gwyneth realised that there was no point in trying to prolong the interview. The town clerk's mind had been made up from the first, and he was not the kind of man to be persuaded of anything. A change of mind was for him a defeat and a humiliation.

'We'll have to think of something else,' said Gwyneth as they left.

By strange coincidence, they saw Aksil Boulifa arriving at the council offices as they left. When he saw them, he gave them a knowing smile, compounded of hostility, contempt and triumph.

'What can he be doing there?' asked Gwyneth.

'Only one thing,' said Ahmed darkly.

When their now-sparse customers were approaching the end of their meals, Ahmed would come up to them and ask them, if they had enjoyed them, to write a good review of the Marrakech on the *Visit Walport* website. Most of them agreed to do so, but such is the frailty of human intention that few did so, and such good reviews as they wrote disappeared mysteriously from the site almost as soon as they appeared, and always below derogatory ones so that by the time any reader reached them, his mind would have been poisoned.

Ahmed and Gwyneth would consult the site angrily for complimentary comments.

Ahmed decided that they should use the same method as Aksil Bouflika and turn the site against the Atlas. But it was not easy: who could they ask to do it? A couple of acquaintances tried, but one evening after what they had written appeared, Aksil Bouflika arrived at the Marrakech and, in front of customers at two tables, accused Ahmed of having written the comments himself to distract from the fact that rats had repeatedly been seen in his kitchen. If he didn't stop his libels, said Aksil, he would do something about it.

'What can he do?' Ahmed said afterwards to his wife, who was near to tears.

Gwyneth though that there was a lot Aksil Boulifa could do, though she wasn't sure exactly what. She waited for the blow to fall, and it was not long in coming.

About a week later, in the afternoon during the quiet part of the day, there came a loud rapping on the locked front door of the Marrakech, as if the whole town were on fire and Ahmed and Gwyneth were being warned to escape.

Ahmed opened the door. The rapping had irritated him. What could have been the justification for it in the absence of fire?

'Yes?' he said as he unlocked and opened the door.

Before him stood a man in his forties dressed in an ill-fitting suit. Behind him stood a younger man in an even worse suit who had a camera. The older man had the face of an unsuccessful predator.

'Health inspection,' he said and whisked from his pocket some kind of identity card. 'We've received reports.'

'What of?' asked Ahmed.

'Breaches,' said the man.

'Breaches? What are those?'

'Breaches — failure to comply with regulations.'

The health inspector spoke to Ahmed as if he were a refractory backward child. Gwyneth came to the door.

'What's going on?' she asked.

'Health inspection,' said the inspector, flashing his identity card again. 'We've had reports.'

'Of what? From whom?'

'I can't tell you that. We have to inspect. We have the right to enter your premises.'

'We have nothing to hide.'

'That's for us to decide.'

The two men entered the Marrakech.

'We must ask you not to watch us,' said the inspector. 'There must be no suspicion of collusion. It would be best if you left for half an hour.'

Ahmed was reluctant to do so, but Gwyneth tugged at his arm.

'Let's do what the man says.'

They returned as suggested in half an hour.

'Well?' said Gwyneth. 'What did you find?'

'I'm not at liberty to say,' said the inspector. 'You'll receive our report in due course.'

A fortnight later arrived a letter that they had to sign for. It notified them that they must close their restaurant forthwith, but they could appeal within ten working days. The inspector's report, which was enclosed, gave the reasons for the order to close. The most damning evidence was that of rat-droppings in many places in the kitchen. They were so numerous that the kitchen must have been overrun with rats. This being the case, said the report, the kitchen of the Marrakesh must never have been swept or cleaned. There was a grave and immediate danger that if the restaurant did not close immediately, there might be an outbreak of leptospirosis which, unrecognised because of its rarity, would lead to deaths. The hygiene of the Marrakech was in general so poor that it was quite beyond sufficient improvement to meet the current standards required.

Ahmed and Gwyneth read the report with mounting fury and disbelief. They had never seen a rat in the kitchen.

'I would've screamed the house down if I'd seen one,' said Gwyneth. 'I'm terrified of rats.'

'They put the droppings there themselves,' said Ahmed. 'Aksil Boulifa is behind this.'

They wrote to the authorities that the evidence against the Marrakech was planted, that they had never seen a rat or its droppings anywhere in the restaurant, and that if they had seen either, they would have done something about it straight away. They received a reply a week later, that they had also to sign for, to the effect that no correspondence about the inspectorate's integrity could be entered into, and therefore that the original order stood to close forthwith the Marrakesh. It must be closed immediately, or the owners would face criminal prosecution.

There was nothing for it but for Ahmed and Gwyneth to obey.

'There is so much prejudice in this country!' said Ahmed. 'Just like in France.'

Although Ahmed's brother had been killed in the civil war in Algeria, which had been Ahmed's original reason for leaving, and there was much corruption there, Ahmed said that it would be better if he and Gwyneth tried their luck in Algeria.